THE DOWN TURN

SNOOK

 AMARQUIS PUBLICATIONS
Amarquis Publications
P.O. Box 34224
North Chesterfield, VA 23234
www.amarquispublications.com

Library of Congress Control Number: 2016903015

ISBN: 978-0-692-65048-6
First Amarquis Publications Paperback Edition March
2016
Printed in the United States

Cover & interior designed by Indie Designz

ACKNOWLEDGEMENTS

I first must give thanks and honor to God, for allowing me to embark on this writing journey. I would like to express my greatest gratitude to my family, friends, and readers. Thank you for all of the support! I'm grateful for those who went with me on this journey during the early stages of this project.

I was inspired to write a story about a family that was affected by the down economy. There are different phases of life and relationships. In this book, you're taken on a journey to see how stress and loss are handled by the characters in this story.

I touched on the subject of breast cancer in this book due to my own personal experience with a breast cancer scare. Breast cancer is a subject that really didn't touch home for me until I found myself in the shoes of many who have experienced the breast cancer scare. Although, I didn't have breast cancer, my tumor had to be removed. I thank God every day for a life cancer free! There are those that are fighting for their lives every day.

To my readers, breast cancer is real and you have to be proactive in knowing the early signs. Support your local and national breast cancer foundations to help bring awareness and to find a cure.

Much love,

Snook

Also by Snook
Issues Of The Heart
The Day The Walls Cried
Karma's Kiss

Coming Soon
Karma's Kiss 2

This book is dedicated to survivors. For those who have weathered the storms of life and are still standing.

THE DOWN TURN

CHAPTER 1

Vivian paced the floor of her bedroom as she waited for her husband, Timothy to return home. Her stomach was in knots. After work, he was supposed to meet co-workers for happy hour at a local bar. Not expecting him home until later, it was now after midnight. She called his cell phone repeatedly with no answer.

"Damn it!" she said, slamming her cell phone down on the nightstand.

She looked at the digital photo frame as it flipped through pictures of the two of them and their three children. Pictures of her once happy life, frozen in time.

Vivian was thirty-five years old. She had a smooth caramel complexion, honey-blonde hair, and a petite frame. She was in the best shape of her life, even after giving birth to twins five years prior.

Each time she thought she heard a car, she raced over to the window to see if it was him. She pulled back the curtains to find that he hadn't returned home. There wasn't a truck in the driveway nor were there any vehicles on the street. She willed him to drive down the street and pull safely into their driveway.

She prayed that he wouldn't be arrested for drinking and driving. In the past, he'd come home a few nights too drunk to have been behind the wheel. Thoughts of a police officer showing up at her front door to inform her that her husband had been in a terrible accident ran through her mind. After her second trip to the bathroom, she decided that pacing the floor and running back and forth from the window wasn't going to bring him home any sooner.

She finally forced herself to bed and said a silent prayer for Timothy's safety as she did most nights like this. She slid under the cool covers. For the second night in a row, she went to bed alone. She looked at Timothy's side of the bed, and she missed the times they went to bed together or joined the other shortly afterward.

He never was one to take a drink before and now he consumed alcohol daily. For the past six months, his drinking increased to daily consumption. Little by little, he started drinking heavily and little by little it changed him.

First, it started with him drinking so much that he would be sprawled out on the bathroom floor with his head in the toilet. He would swear before God that he wouldn't drink again. However, after a few days of feeling better, he would have another drink. The next stage was him drinking so much that he would come home late or not all. He blamed it on the alcohol.

In recent months, he had become more distant. When he would drink, he became angry. He would lash out at Vivian and become aggressive.

Timothy stumbled into the house at two o'clock in the morning. He did so while knocking over furniture as he made his way around the house cursing at the top of his lungs. The sound of glass breaking startled Vivian out of her sleep.

Timothy was dark-skinned, tall, with a muscular frame. Wearing a bald head ever since the young age of thirty-eight, he towered over Vivian's petite frame.

"Vivian, where you at? Get your ass up and hear what your man has to say! I've been working all day and no hot meal is on the table. Get your ass out here woman!" he slurred.

Vivian couldn't believe that he came in not only late, but noisy. She jumped out of the bed and grabbed her robe. She was sure the neighbors could hear his rant.

"What do you think you're doing? Your children are sleeping," she said in a low, but serious tone, trying not to wake the children.

Noticing that he'd knocked over a lamp, she saw the broken pieces and the bulb's glass shattered all over the hardwood floor.

"Don't bring my kids into this! What have you done all day? Where is my dinner?"

Vivian moved from her bedroom door into the living room where she hoped the kids wouldn't be able to hear them. Timothy followed her closely almost stepping on the back of her heels.

"Dinner? Dinner was hours ago. It's two o'clock in the morning! You're drunk and need to calm down."

"Bitch, I've been working all damn day, and you couldn't have dinner for me when I come home?" he asked, pointing a finger in her face.

Vivian tightened the knot on her robe feeling very uncomfortable with his aggression towards her. She looked away from him feeling inadequate for a moment.

It was true, she didn't bring in the money that paid the bills, but she brought in something. She kept a clean house and took care of the children. This was the first time he threw this in her face and it hurt.

"I've been working, too. Maybe not as hard as you, but I do work. I keep this house in order, clean up after you and your children, cook dinner every night, and I still manage to be a wife to your sorry ass. I do all of this while you're out drinking your life away. You don't even see that your family is slipping right through your fingers. I can't take you having these alcoholic binges. You know that my mother was an alcoholic and what that did to me as I child. I'm not going to let you take my children through that!"

"Fuck that! I want my food on the table when I get home. You sit on your lazy ass all day doing nothing. Did you feed my kids!" he shouted.

Vivian looked at him with disgust, realizing that he didn't understand anything she just said.

My father always said you couldn't argue with a drunk. You will lose every time.

"I'm a bitch? You're not going to disrespect me like this in my house."

She tried to pass him, but he blocked her pathway with his body. She turned to walk the other way, but he pulled her to him.

"Bitch, you think this your house? This is my damn house. I pay the bills up in here you cunt!" he spat in her face.

Alcohol filled her nostrils. Her stomach turned. Vivian yanked away from the tight grip he had on both her arms and stepped back from him. She was hurt by his words, drunk or not. Her heart began to pound in her chest.

"You alcoholic fucker! You have got to be out your damn mind! If you call me anything other than Vivian, you're going to be sorry!" she yelled.

She backed away slowly as he wobbled towards her. Slob dripped from his bottom lip and hung from his face. She was disgusted with him. She walked around the back of the sofa, away from Timothy and towards her bedroom.

"Where the hell do you think you're going?"

"I'm going to bed, and you need to sleep that shit off!" she said.

"Get your ass back in here and fix me something to eat! I'm hungry!"

"Fuck you!"

Vivian retreated to her bedroom as she locked herself behind the door that separated her from Timothy's drunken rage.

After banging and knocking on the door, Timothy said the most painful words, "I wish I never married you."

That night, she cried herself to sleep asking God, *Why?*

Those words had been the cause of her lack of focus and headaches. Finances were strained by the price of gas, food, and other necessities skyrocketing. Vivian found a part time job working at a local electronic store selling computers that she could work three days a week while the kids were in school.

She enjoyed her job. The pay wasn't much, but she didn't have much choice. People were being laid off at a faster rate than they were being hired.

She obtained a master's degree in human resource management years ago, but had been out of work since having the twins. She had planned to go back to work once the twins started school, but couldn't find a job.

Timothy had a degree in information technology and was a software engineer for Smith and Simmons Global. He worked hard to get into the company. Since being there, he received many accolades for his work.

It was his idea that she quit her job and stay at home with the twins. Even when she said that she would rather go back to work to help him with the bills, he still insisted. Now that he threw it back in her face, she knew she had to get back to full time employment and bring in more money. She hoped this would be enough to take some of the strain off the marriage.

CHAPTER 2

"Come on kids. Hurry up and finish your breakfast so that we can get going," Vivian called out from the living room where she was gathering the children's coats and backpacks.

They had pancakes, sausage, and strawberries for breakfast. It was seven-thirty in the morning and they were running twenty minutes behind schedule.

Timothy was the first from the table leaving their three children, ten year old Dominic, and five year old twins, Demetrius and Journey. Journey was a spitting image of her mother and Demetrius was the male version of her. Dominic took after his father with his smooth dark skin and dark curly hair.

Vivian watched Timothy's every move as he kissed his children and headed for the front door. She made her way over to her husband.

"I love you, honey. See you guys later," he said.

Timothy softly kissed his wife's reluctant lips. She didn't return the kiss, keeping her lips pressed together. She stepped back from him.

"Are you sure about that?" she asked looking into his eyes.

"I don't have time for that this morning. I can't continue to leave here stressed and go to work every day. A man has enough to worry about out here!" he said with fire in his eyes.

He squinted his hazel eyes as he peered down at her. Anger melted from his face.

"Last night will be the last time you disrespect me, Timothy. You have been coming in here all hours of the night and losing respect for me as your wife. I'm not tolerating that any longer in this marriage," she said sternly.

"I'm sorry about last night. I had a little too much to drink. I don't know what I said or did, but I'm sorry."

He took a deep, uneven breath.

"If you're so sorry, then stop doing shit to be sorry for!" she said through clenched teeth.

The two of them glared at each other, refusing to be the first one to back down. After a short stare down, Timothy brushed against Vivian, shoving her back slightly and knocking her off balance. She turned around expecting an apology, but he walked out the door and slammed it behind him, leaving her standing alone.

Her blood boiled with anger as she started toward the door demanding an apology. She shook her head in disbelief. As soon as she reached the door, she heard him speed out of the driveway.

Vivian's heart was crushed. She couldn't believe his actions toward her. He left her feeling hurt and alone. She fought back tears as she took in a deep breath and slowly blew it out. Finally, she regained her composure.

Vivian shook her head and headed for the kitchen to move the children along. She was stopped in her tracks by a sharp pain that raced across her forehead. She closed her eyes and waited for the pain to subside. A few seconds later, the pain left as fast as it had come.

Continuing with her daily routine, she stopped suddenly as she saw the children wore a look of distress on their faces. It was apparent that they witnessed the two of them once again in a heated encounter, which took place far too often.

"I'm done. Why are you and daddy fighting again?" Journey asked.

She managed to get the syrup from the pancakes in her hair as she played with the stringy stickiness she created.

"Mom, look what Journey did!" Demetrius said pointing to his twin sister.

"He spilled syrup on his clothes!" Journey shot back.

The two of them stood in front of Vivian pointing at each other. He too managed to make a mess of his own. His white collar shirt had two large stains on the front and drops of syrup stained his khakis.

"Oh, my goodness, Demetrius! How did you do that?" she asked in frustration.

Demetrius needed a complete change of clothes, which would cause them to run further behind schedule. Her headache intensified. She needed an aspirin. Recently, with the stress of married life came the headaches.

"Dominic, please help me with your brother. Take him to the bathroom to wash his hands and face," she requested of her ten year old son.

She felt bad for asking him to help.

"Okay, come on Demetrius," Dominic said.

He moved sluggishly to his mother's request.

"Thanks."

She attempted to shake off a relentless headache as Dominic led his brother to the nearby bathroom.

Vivian sat next to Journey, who was still fighting with the syrupy strings of hair that kept sticking to her face and hands.

"Mommy," Journey whined.

"Hold on, baby."

She rubbed her temples in an attempt to relieve the pain.

Dominic returned with Demetrius in tow. He picked up the plates from the table and walked over to the sink. He rinsed the dishes and placed them in the dishwasher.

"Thanks, Dominic. Now get on your jackets and backpacks while I get your sister cleaned up."

Vivian led Journey to the bathroom where syrup handprints stained the door and sink. She retrieved her aspirin from the medicine cabinet and filled a glass with water. After taking two aspirins, she placed the bottle in her pocket for later.

"Journey, let's get you all cleaned up."

She tickled Journey's stomach causing her to fall into her arms in laughter. She cleaned her face and wiped her hair with a wet cloth.

"Ouch, it hurts!" Journey cried out.

Vivian brushed her now wet hair into a single ponytail.

"You shouldn't have gotten syrup in your hair. Now hold still."

After she finished combing Journey's hair and Demetrius was changed, she was another fifteen minutes behind schedule. She rushed Journey out the bathroom, pulling her by the arm.

"Let's go!" she called out.

She frantically pulled on Journey's back bag and then Demetrius'.

"Dominic, do you have everything you need for school?"

"Yes, ma'am."

Vivian put on her coat and headed for the door, but remembered that she forgot her keys hanging in the kitchen.

"Damn it!" she said, as she ran back to the kitchen to retrieve her keys.

She thought out her route trying to avoid buses that may hold her up any further. She opted for the highway, which she rarely took in the mornings. This would shave about ten minutes off her drive.

Finally, in the car, the children sat quietly. Vivian turned on the radio to settle in for the drive. *Amazing Grace*, her mother's favorite song was playing. A chill ran up her spine. Every time she heard the song, she always thought back to her childhood.

Vivian thought back to the days when her mother would be so drunk that she couldn't care for her. She recalled one morning when she was nine years old and was getting ready for school. Her mother was still asleep and she had gotten up to dress herself. She quietly shuffled through her closet for an outfit and chose a pair of light blue jeans and a pink sweater. Her mother had chosen a floral dress and white tights for her to wear. She hung the dress on the closet door still in the plastic from the cleaners. Vivian hated wearing dresses. She ironed her clothes and brushed her hair into two pigtails tied with a pink ribbon.

Her mother called out to her, "Vivian, are you dressed for school, baby?"

"Yes, ma'am," she answered hiding in her room.

"Make sure you stay clean today. Your father is taking us out for dinner."

"Yes, ma'am."

Vivian stood very still. She didn't want her mother to

call her into her bedroom and see that she didn't have on the dress she picked out for her.

She thought about her father. The best part of the day was when her father met her at the bus stop every afternoon. Each time, he would bring her a piece of candy to eat before dinner. The thoughts put a smile on her face.

"Vivian?" her mother called out again.

"Yes, ma'am?"

She moved to the front door and slowly turned the knob.

"Come here and let me see you," her mother slurred.

Vivian slowly walked down the hall to her mother's bedroom as the smell of liquor and piss filled her lungs. Her father moved into the spare bedroom when her mother's drinking worsened four months earlier. Her mother was sitting on the side of the bed. Her once white nightgown hung off her shoulders exposing her frail body. The auburn curly locks that normally fell passed her shoulders were matted to her head.

"Lift your head little girl. What's the matter with you? I know you're not ashamed of me. Are you?"

"No, ma'am, I'm not. I just wished that you wouldn't drink so much sometimes."

Her mother drank every day.

"I know, baby. I'm sick."

"I know."

"Look at your hair. Let me brush it for you. What happened to the dress?"

"I didn't want to wear a dress today."

Vivian walked over and sat between her mother's legs on the floor. She held her breath as her mother brushed through her hair while humming, *Amazing Grace*. Her mother had a beautiful voice. It was soothing to have her mother's loving hands in her hair.

Vivian swore to never be like her mother. If she were to have a drink, she would know her limit. She vowed to be a better mother to her children than her mother was to her. She especially devoted her time to build a relationship with her daughter; one she never had with her mother growing up. She knew how important a mother was to a daughter. She loved all her children and reminded them of that daily.

CHAPTER 3

It was a beautiful morning. There were clear blue skies and the sun shined brightly. School buses lined the street ready to turn into the bus circle. Parents waited impatiently for the officer to give them permission to turn into the school's drop off zone. She followed the line of cars.

"Don't forget your backpacks. Have a good day. I love you!" Vivian said.

The children unbuckled their seat belts and exited the car. They all returned the love and rushed towards the school. Vivian sat in her car and smiled at her eager children. They were always excited about school and it showed in their grades. They were all scholars.

Vivian sat in her car and breathed deeply as she watched the children walk into school. The morning had been tougher than usual, because of the extra load she carried. Something was going on with Timothy, but she just couldn't put her finger on it. She didn't know him anymore. The drinking was turning him into a stranger.

Vivian was running late for work. The traffic was backed up into the street from where she needed to turn. She pulled into the parking lot. As usual, the delivery truck pulled in front of the store, blocking the entrance causing cars to maneuver around carelessly. Vivian drove around the truck in her champagne Lexus and found parking, but not before almost having a head-on collision with another car leaving the parking lot.

"Get out of the way! I know you see this truck parked here!" Vivian shouted at the other driver.

The driver laid on his horn as she gave him the finger.

Pulling down the visor, she flipped the mirror up and checked her makeup. She added a layer of lip gloss to her lips. She combed her bangs and smoothed her hair back into a neat ponytail before stepping out of the car.

"Good morning, Mr. Ming," Vivian said with a huge smile on her face.

This was her time away from home with no kids, husband, or dishes. She sashayed her petite frame down the aisle with her long honey-blonde ponytail swinging from side-to-side.

"There are three laptops to setup by noon," Mr. Ming said, as soon as she entered the office.

Mr. Ming was the store owner and her boss.

"Good morning to you, too," Vivian said sarcastically.

"If you say so," Mr. Ming replied.

She rolled her eyes and slammed her keys on the desk.

"Why do you always have an attitude when I come in here?"

Not expecting an answer, she proceeded to clock in.

"No attitude. You just work!" he yelled.

"Okay, I work and you pay," she said mocking Mr. Ming's accent. "I'll pray for you."

She shook her head in disbelief of his sudden mood swings.

Since his wife became ill and unable to help at the store, he had become irate with everyone. Mr. Ming stormed out of the office, but not without giving Vivian the nastiest look his face could conjure.

"Asshole," she mumbled.

Mrs. Ming was a beautiful and kind woman who would give her last to someone if they needed it. No one knew exactly what was wrong with Mrs. Ming, but they all prayed that she would recover and soon.

It was two-thirty and Vivian was setting up her last computer for a waiting customer when her cell phone vibrated in her pants pocket. She ignored the phone and continued working. Seconds later, the office phone rang. She was due to clock out in fifteen minutes and needed to pickup her children from school.

"Hello, thanks for calling…" she began before being cut off.

"Viv, I need you to come home now," Timothy said in a low tone.

"Tim, is everything all right?" she asked nervously.

"Just get home as soon as you can," he said and hung up the phone.

She panicked and immediately began to shake nervously. She immediately thought something happened to one of the children or her parents. Her heart began to pound inside of her chest. Vivian had no clue what was going on. She checked her cell phone. Timothy was supposed to be at work, but he called her cell from the house phone. Something was wrong. She sat the laptop to the side and gathered her things to leave.

She felt lost. She remembered when her mother came to her middle school unexpectedly. She was called to the office. Her mother and grandmother were there in tears.

"What's wrong? What happened?" she asked frantically.

"It's your father. He's in the hospital," her grandmother said.

Just when she thought her parents were finally getting somewhere, her father suffered a heart attack. While her mother was in a ninety-day treatment center for depression and alcohol addiction, her father moved back into their bedroom. He prepared for her return and reminded Vivian every day that things were going to be the way they used to be before her mother became sick. Her mother was now four months sober and things were taking a turn for the worse for them.

Walking quickly out the office, she ran into Mr. Ming.

"Sorry, Mr. Ming, I have to leave now. It's an emergency."

She knew how much he hated employees to leave early, but she didn't care what he had to say about it, because she was leaving anyway.

"That's fine. See you Monday," he said continuing on his way.

Vivian watched him walk away slumped over with his head hung low. Not expecting this reaction, she was now concerned for Mr. Ming. Something was terribly wrong and she was sure it had something to do with Mrs. Ming's health. She dashed out of the store.

She headed for the kids school weaving in and out of traffic. She arrived just as she saw Timothy loading the children into his Ford F-150. She laid on the horn as she pulled two cars behind them.

"What are you doing?" she yelled, leaping from her car and running to Timothy's truck. He turned to find a frantic Vivian almost in tears.

"The kids are fine. I thought I told you to meet me at the house."

"That's all you said. I didn't know if something happened to one of the kids. What in the hell is going on? You're scaring me." She placed her hands on his chest and pleaded for an explanation. "Please, tell me what's wrong? I can't take this. I need to know what's going on."

"There is something I have to tell you. Just follow me to the house. I don't want to upset the kids."

"Mommy, I want to go with you!" Journey called out.

Journey tried to open the door, but the child safety lock prevented the door from opening.

"Me, too!" Demetrius said crawling over Journey and towards the door.

"Sit down, Demetrius!" Dominic yelled.

Timothy looked into the truck.

"Mommy forgot I told her that I would pick you up from school today. I'm going to take you home and mommy is going to meet us there." He lied to comfort the children.

She looked at the back window and saw the twin's faces up against the window, watching them. Realizing that the children were watching, she forced a smile. She looked through the window to find her three babies staring back at her with concern. After blowing three kisses to them, she walked back to her car. Tears fell from her eyes, blurring her vision as she trailed her husband's truck to their home.

She knew that bad news was definitely coming her way. Timothy never picked up the children from school.

Is there a death in the family?

Both vehicles pulled into the driveway, side-by-side. She immediately noticed the Halloween decorations. Timothy must have been home for a while. The scarecrow door hanger, inflatable pumpkin, and a haunted house were on the lawn. Journey was the first to leap from the truck.

"Mommy!" Journey yelled, running to Vivian.

She hugged her tightly. She always sensed when something was wrong.

"Hi, honey. How was your day?" Vivian asked.

"It was good," Journey answered.

"Hi, Vivian," Demetrius said, reaching for a hug.

"Hi, Demetrius," she said accepting him into her arms.

She ignored the fact the he called her by her first name. Any other day, she would correct him and force him to address her properly.

"Come on guys. Let's get a snack," Timothy said, rushing everyone into the house. He wore a look of distress on his face, which made Vivian even more nervous.

Vivian followed the children to the kitchen where they found fresh fruit and assorted crackers waiting for them.

How long has he been home?

Vivian followed Timothy to their bedroom. He closed the door behind them. She turned to him and placed her hands on his chest, and searched his eyes.

"What's wrong?" she asked.

"Please sit down so we can talk."

He took her hand and led her over to their bed. A hint of Vodka floated up her nose; something she hadn't noticed before.

"Really? Are you drinking this early in the day? You've been drinking and you had our children in the car with you!" she yelled, yanking away from him in disgust.

"I lost my job today. They laid off over half of the staff," he said in shame.

"What? How could they do this? They could've at least given you some sort of notice so that you could've looked for another job!" she said in shock, forgetting about the argument at hand.

"They can do whatever they want. They don't care anything about our homes or our families," he said.

"What are we going to do? My job isn't enough to pay our bills."

She paced the floor. She began to cry, relieved that there wasn't death in the family, but sad that their finances were going to be little to nothing.

Timothy reached for her, pulling her beside him on the bed. He held her in his arms as she cried. He rubbed her in an attempt to soothe her. She was scared and didn't know what to do.

"I will find work. Don't worry about it. We still have savings," he assured her.

"Savings? How long are we supposed to live off savings? We only have a few thousand left. That's not enough to pay the mortgage for more than four months."

"I will receive some sort of severance pay. I have worked there for over fifteen years. That has got to count for something."

"Yeah, it's worth putting you out in the cold."

"Don't blame me for this! I can't control this economy and what's happened. People are being laid off and losing their homes every day!" he yelled.

Not wanting to fight, Vivian stood up to leave the room before things escalated. When Timothy drank, he became defensive and aggressive.

"I wasn't blaming you. I'm just upset. Let's talk about this later."

She reached for the door.

"You're upset? I lost my job, not you! How do you think I feel?"

Timothy stood between her and the door.

"I don't know. You tell me," she said, looking him in his red eyes. "From the smell of things, you should be feeling..." she started.

Before she could complete her sentence, Timothy grabbed both her arms and pinned her against the wall.

"I drink, because you drive me crazy with your nagging and sarcasm. I've been hearing rumors for months about this layoff, but I couldn't come home and talk to you about it. You're always complaining about something. That's why I drink!" he spat in her face.

Vivian once again felt the pain from his words. He couldn't talk to her about what was going on so he drank. She felt guilty and partly responsible for his drinking.

Vivian turned her face away from him to avoid the direct hit from his alcohol fumed spit. The smell of his breath made her stomach turn. She gathered the strength to push him backward causing him to stumble over.

She seized the opportunity to escape the bedroom. She hurried out, slamming the door quickly behind her. When she turned around, she was startled by Journey standing there with tear filled eyes.

"Why are you fighting?" she asked through her sobs.

"We are not fighting honey. We were just talking about grown up things," she lied.

"I heard daddy yelling at you."

Vivian knelt down and wiped Journey's tears. She fought back tears from the pain of seeing her daughter hurt.

"He wasn't yelling at me. Everything is all right. Now, get your homework so that I can help you."

Vivian couldn't believe the stress that she was under in her marriage of sixteen years. She didn't know how to handle the sudden changes in her marriage. The alcohol turned him into another person. He was disrespectful and insensitive.

Now facing more of a financial hardship, it was sure to further strain the marriage. She thought back to when they first married. They had to start out like every young couple with a small apartment, used furniture, and a tight budget. Over the years, they accomplished much together and never turned their backs on each other.

Things were so good for so long, that she hadn't prayed and asked God for much. Now, she found herself saying silent prayers every chance she had. Her life was quickly changing and her future was uncertain. She prayed that God would keep her family intact.

CHAPTER 4

Raindrops pounded heavily on the shingled roof of their modern brick rancher. On a warm rainy summer's night, Vivian would stand under the portico and take in the fresh rain. The downpour made its way through the gutters and down the spouts. The house was quiet. All that could be heard was thunder at a distance and the house glowed with the lightning.

Vivian woke up in Journey's bed where she last read her a bedtime story. It was ten-thirty p.m. on the Hello Kitty wall clock. Journey was sleeping along with Demetrius in the bed beside her. She kissed both her children and watched them sleep peacefully.

"I love how you love our children," Timothy said from the doorway startling her.

She turned to look at him with sadness in her eyes. She hated seeing him that way. His eyes were red and he stank of liquor. She approached him cautiously.

"What's happening to us? What's going on with you and this drinking?"

She searched his eyes for the answer.

"I don't know. I guess it's just life. I promise you that I'll fix this. I had my last drink, Vivian," he said, as sincerely as the alcohol would allow him.

"I don't want to fight you all the time. I just want my husband back. All this fighting is affecting the children. We can't continue to do this."

She threw her arms around him.

"I know and that's why I'm leaving for Charlotte to find work. Once we get back on our feet, everything will be okay."

"What? Charlotte is in North Carolina!" she shouted, and then she let go of him.

She was reminded that the children were asleep when Demetrius turned over in his bed. She lowered her voice and closed the door behind her.

"What the hell do you mean you're leaving?" she asked angrily.

"Right now, I don't have a job. I'm going there to find work. Once I find a job, I'll send for you and the kids."

"What about our home? All of our family is here in Richmond."

"What do you want me to do? My family is in Charlotte too so you'll still have help with the children if you need it. My cousin said there are jobs in my field. I will make more money and we can sell the house. I promise you that if things don't pan out in a month, I'll come back here and try something else."

Vivian looked at him as if he'd lost his mind. She couldn't believe he wanted to desert them in a sinking ship. She didn't understand why he had to go so far to find work and leave her behind. She was hurt and exchanging words with him wasn't going to change that.

She left him standing in the hallway alone. She went into their bedroom.

The room felt as if it were spinning. She held onto her dresser and took in deep breaths. She regained her composure. Looking in the mirror, she noticed the dark bags under her eyes. Moving closer to the mirror, she poked at them in hopes of making them disappear. She sighed.

She ran a hot shower and undressed. The steam filled the room as she caught the last glimpses of her reflection in the mirror.

Stepping into the shower, she flinched at the heat coming from the water. She allowed the hot water to fall down over her head, stinging her skin. Her stomach muscles contracted as the hot water beat down on her naked body.

A cool breeze entered the shower as she heard the door open and close. She felt her husband's presence in the bathroom with her.

She stood still. Timothy pulled back the shower curtain and stepped in with her. No words were exchanged. He pulled her close to him kissing her softly at first and then more passionately. She wrapped her legs around his waist as he lifted and positioned her for entry. The hot water beat down on them both as they took their pain out on each other.

After making love to her husband, there was peace between the two of them. She wished that things could go back to the way they used to be. She missed times like this when she would lay in his arms feeling loved and safe.

CHAPTER 5

The next morning, Vivian woke up to an empty bed. She rolled over and ran her hand down the cold sheets where Timothy was supposed to be. A wide smile crossed her face as she thought about the long night of lovemaking. Proceeding to get up from the bed, she was stricken by a sharp pain in her head. She sat back down and realized that stress, marital issues, and finances were still there despite her attempts of washing them away.

She headed for the kitchen with her migraine medication to find the kitchen filled with thick smoke. Timothy and the children greeted her.

"Good morning!" they all yelled.

"Good morning. Open up a window before we choke to death."

Her eyes began to burn.

"Good morning, sweetheart," Timothy said.

She searched for the kid's faces through the smoke.

The fire alarm began to sound off. She opened the patio doors and kitchen windows quickly releasing the smoke.

"Kids, wait in your rooms until your father is finished burning down the house."

"The one morning I decide to get up and cook breakfast, I burn it all up," Timothy said.

Vivian walked over and hugged him while peeking in the pan of burnt eggs and another of greasy sausage.

"Leave the cooking to me," she said with a laugh. "Did you get the paper?"

"No."

He dumped the burnt eggs in the trash can.

Vivian walked to the front door to get the newspaper. At the door sat a suitcase and a duffel bag. Vivian was confused as to why bags were at the front door. She didn't expect Timothy to leave so soon. She headed back to the kitchen.

"Whose bags are at the door?" she asked curiously.

"Mine. I thought I might head down to North Carolina this weekend. No sense in waiting," he said hesitantly.

"Really? So this is another one of those decisions you just make by yourself," she said sarcastically.

"Why wait? The sooner I get down there, the better."

"Don't you think this is a decision that we should've made together?"

"You already knew my plans. I just decided to move things up. You were right about not having enough savings, so I thought I better go ahead and get started."

Vivian stared at the stranger in the kitchen wondering what went wrong in their marriage. The lines of communication were nonexistent.

How could he make such decisions on his own? Doesn't he realize that his decisions affect all of us?

It seemed that she lost a small piece of him each day.

"This isn't going to work for me. We are supposed to be married and talk to each other about things like this. You're not supposed to make a decision like this without talking to me first."

"What are you saying?"

"I just don't understand how you can just pick up and leave."

"I'm not leaving you. I'm trying to find work, that's all. Once things pan out, I'll send for you and the kids," he assured her again.

"And if things don't?"

"Well, I guess that's another conversation to have."

In the back of Vivian's mind, she felt that things weren't going to work out. Feeling that there was more going on with Timothy, Vivian knew he wasn't going to tell her. She had to get back to work and come up with a *Plan B*. Since his mind was made up, she decided to let it go.

The love that was once shared had faded over the years, but she still loved him. She just wasn't in love with the person he had become. There was always the possibility of one day becoming a single parent, but she didn't expect it to be today.

CHAPTER 6

Two weeks had passed since Timothy decided to leave for North Carolina. He was due to start his new job any day. Now making ten thousand more dollars than his last job plus bonuses. Things were looking up. He knew that Vivian and the children missed him dearly. He looked forward to their nightly calls right before bed.

He had been staying at the *Westin Hotel* in Charlotte due to its uptown location. The hotel was very nice and Timothy was starting to let living in Charlotte sink in. He couldn't wait to take his boys to the *NASCAR Hall of Fame*.

The television's volume was low so he could hear what was going on around him. The sound coming from the hallway stopped short of his door. He sat up anticipating a knock. After a few seconds, he relaxed, thinking that he was mistaken. Just as he sat back down, he heard a soft knock at the door. His stomach turned as he walked to open it.

"Hi," his boss Samantha Carter said.

Samantha was stunning as usual. She had long brown hair and hazel eyes. Her small frame and round hips complimented her tall frame. She wore five-inch leopard print stilettos and a black pantsuit with a red belt that complimented her small waist. The red lipstick she wore matched her long manicured nails. As she walked into the room uninvited, she let her hair down out of the bun it was pulled into.

"Hi," Timothy said dryly.

He headed back towards the bed, but decided to sit in the chair.

"You don't seem happy to see me. Why haven't you been answering my calls? What's the matter? After all that I've done for you. You weren't the only one laid off. I was, too. I told you about the layoff and I found you this job. I did all of this for us. Now, I think you should be more appreciative."

After inspecting it carefully, she sat on the bed.

"All of this was your idea. I didn't want it this way. I never wanted to leave my wife and children. What happened between us was a mistake," he said through clenched teeth.

"A mistake? Well, if you feel that way, you can pack up and run back home to your little wife. Or, you can get your mind right and stay here with your job and me. There is nothing back there for you. You were about to be broke and unemployed. I have you all set up here in Charlotte. With me, your job is secure. I promise," she said.

She eyed Timothy seductively. He hated that the worse he treated her, the more she seemed to want him. He didn't know what to do with her.

"You can't make me do this. My family is supposed to be here with me. I didn't agree to this," he said angrily.

"Did you really think you were calling the shots? No sir, I am. Listen, I have an appointment for you to meet with an attorney to file for your divorce."

"I'm not leaving my wife!" he shouted, and then stood to his feet.

"Yes, you are. If not, then I will make sure that she leaves you. Don't forget about our home video we made. I must say, that was one of your finest performances."

She leaned back on the bed and licked her red lips seductively.

"What video? I didn't make a sex tape with you!" he shouted.

He thought about how stupid he was for letting a woman tape him having sex and he didn't know. He balled up his fists in anger wanting to punch her in the face for threatening his family.

"Oh, we made a video."

"I didn't know you were taping us. Where is it?" he yelled again.

"Oh, but you did know that we were fucking right? It's in a safe place just in case I need it." She laughed and slammed a business card down on the nightstand.

"If you go anywhere near my wife, I will kill you."

Timothy's blood pressure rose as his fist became tighter.

"I'm not playing games with you. If you want your job, then be there. If you want to be broke and lonely, then go back home."

Samantha stood to her feet. Timothy grabbed her from behind and put his arm around her neck. He squeezed tightly as she clawed at his hands and face. She struggled to get him to release her.

He was fueled by anger. He thought how easy it was for him to snap her skinny neck and rid himself of her. Then reality set in. If he killed this white woman in his hotel room, he would be under the jail. She kicked the wall sending them both to the floor, releasing her from his grip. They were both out of breath.

They stared at each other panting for air. Timothy was the first to his feet. He could see the fear in her enlarged hazel eyes as he approached her as she lay on the floor. He picked her up by her throat and dragged her to the front door. She grabbed for his face, scratching him and drawing blood.

"This is over. I'm going home. Do you understand?" he asked her for confirmation.

He pulled her so close that he inhaled her short breaths.

Samantha's eyes bulged. She nodded her head as she tried to breathe through the tight grip he had around her neck. When he let go of her, she fell to the floor gasping for air. He looked at the clock and it was almost 8:30 p.m. It was time for the kids to call before they went to bed.

He allowed her a few more minutes to catch her breath before opening the door and pushing her out. She ran to the elevators in tears. He waited until she was on the elevator before going into his room. He wanted to kill her for threatening his marriage. He didn't want to have to lie to Vivian or the children anymore. He regretted ever getting himself in this situation. He took in deep breaths to slow his breathing. Just like clockwork, his cell phone rang.

"Hi, baby," Vivian said in her sexiest voice.

"Hey, you," Timothy replied.

Her voice immediately calmed him.

"The kids turned in early tonight so it's just me and you. I'm wearing absolutely nothing," she purred into the phone.

The sound of Vivian's voice resonated in his ear sending tingling sensations throughout his body. Timothy's blood rushed to his penis making it harden through his jeans. He began to rub himself.

"She misses you so much. She has so much to tell you," she whispered.

"He misses her more," he moaned.

Unzipping his jeans, he pulled out his erect penis. He began stroking himself as he visualized her naked body.

"Tell me what you're doing now," she said.

Timothy was startled by someone yelling and banging on his door.

"Who is that?" Vivian asked.

"Let me call you back. It's the hotel manager," he said.

He leaped from the bed and remembered to put his penis back in his pants. As he rushed to open the door, he tripped on a leopard print purse that was on the floor. He cracked the door open to see who it was and noticed it was Samantha. He was glad that it wasn't the police.

Swinging open the door, he found a teary-eyed Samantha standing there rubbing the bruises that formed around her neck.

"What were you doing?" she asked through her sobs.

She stepped slowly into the room trying to stay as far away from Timothy as possible. She looked down at his hard on.

"None of your damn business. Now get your shit and get out!" Timothy said angrily.

"I left my purse."

Arching her back as deep as she could, she leaned down and picked up her purse while looking back at Timothy.

"There you have it. I need to finish packing my things," he said nervously.

Samantha's plump ass was turning him on, but he fought back the thought of throwing her over the bed and giving her what she wanted. She knew what she was doing.

"Oh, here are the keys to the apartment."

She dangled a set of shiny gold keys in his face. He didn't move. Samantha tossed the keys on the dresser. He didn't respond. Samantha headed out of the door that was still being held by Timothy.

"Next time you want to rub one out, you should call me."

Timothy slammed the door and mumbled, "Bitch."

He went back to pick up his cell phone to call Vivian back, but she was still on the phone. He gasped at the sight of the active call on his phone. He stared at the phone in disbelief. As his heart pounded in his chest, Timothy didn't know what or how much she'd heard. He contemplated just hanging up on her.

"Timothy!" Vivian yelled through the phone, snapping him out of a trance.

"Vivian, I'm sorry. That was the hotel manager."

"Save it, Timothy. Hotel manager my ass! I know just who that was. How long have you been sleeping with her?" Vivian asked in a calm even tone.

The sound of those words grabbed his heart and refused to let go. He was scared and didn't want to lose his wife and children.

"I need to talk to you in person, not over the phone," Timothy said.

He was now up and pacing the floor. There was no doubt where the conversation was going. Knowing Vivian, she was already dialing the attorney's number.

"I have my answer!" she said through tears.

Vivian hung up the phone.

"I hate these damn phones. Fuck!" he yelled.

Timothy threw his cell phone at the wall and paced the floor angrily.

CHAPTER 7

Vivian grabbed her robe off the bed and wrapped it tightly around her naked body. Sobbing, she felt used after showering and laying there butt naked to have phone sex with her husband.

"Oh, my God! I can't believe him!" she cried hysterically.

Biting the pillow to muffle her cries, she curled into a fetal position and began to feel nauseous.

"First, the drinking and now another woman! I should've known something wasn't right with him. It all makes sense now," she said aloud.

Her heart ached with pain. She grabbed her chest and tried to rub it away. It didn't help at all. She poured her pain into the pillow, which was now soaked with tears. With every tear shed, she let go of the pieces that were left of him.

"The bastard has the nerve to have another woman! After I cooked, cleaned, and washed his filthy underwear for all these years!" she ranted.

He owed her an explanation. Vivian decided to call him back to see exactly what he had to say. Her small hands trembled as she dialed his number. Emotions ripped through her body and settled in her chest.

"Hello, now where were we?" Timothy asked.

"At the part where she left her purse in your hotel room," Vivian said coldly.

"The hotel manager was in here earlier," he began.

"Save it. That wasn't the hotel manager. I know that voice."

"What voice?" he asked nervously.

"That was Samantha. She has called this house enough over the years for me to know her voice very well," Vivian explained.

"What are you talking about? When did she call?"

He began to stumble over his words.

"She always seemed to call when you weren't home. She'd claimed that you weren't answering your cell and you were needed back at the office. Have you been having an affair with your boss?" she asked calmly.

She tried her hardest not to snap. She wanted to get the information she needed. The phone became quiet. She knew he was debating on whether or not he should lie or tell the truth.

"Vivian, it isn't what you think," he protested.

"I had my suspicions, but I didn't think you would do this to us. When I found the birthday card she sent you last year with the hearts drawn on them I knew she wanted you. When I asked you about it, you downplayed it. Samantha? This woman has been in our home and around our children. She was invited to our dinner parties and our children's birthday parties. You were fucking her!"

"No, just let me explain. I never meant to hurt you. I'm so sorry."

"So am I, for putting all of my trust in you. Trusting that you would do right by me and this family was my biggest mistake!" Vivian yelled.

Vivian ended the conversation with those words. Although he didn't admit to anything, she didn't need him to. She heard enough and had enough. She was hurt, but she felt liberated somehow. All the stress of the marriage was going to end, but not quite how she imagined. She loved her husband, but quickly saw the love fade right before her eyes. Reality set in as she thought about her children, home, and bills. Oh, how life was going to change.

Vivian tried to place blame on herself.

Was I a good wife to him? Maybe I should've listened to him more? I should've shown him more attention.

She quickly washed those thoughts away. Timothy had never given her a reason not to trust him. It wasn't until recently that his behavior changed with the drinking. Even then, she didn't think that it was another woman.

It was the end of her marriage. Besides the paperwork, custody, and support issues, she had to learn to be alone. She had another option and that was to stay and work things out. She thought that working things out was helping him with drinking, but having an affair was nothing for her to work out. She just wasn't accepting it and she'd had enough.

CHAPTER 8

After crying herself to sleep, Vivian found herself wanting to put on her clothes and drive to Charlotte to fuck Timothy up for pulling that bullshit on her. She was amazed that he could treat her that after all the love she'd given him. All the years of marriage and that still wasn't enough.

She was almost convinced that all men really did cheat. That was something she didn't allow herself to believe. Timothy was the last man she thought would cheat on her. That was why she married him, and she had the whole idea of love and the happily ever after. Now, she knew there was no happily ever after for them.

She couldn't be sure, but knowing him, he was probably on his way to plead his case. There was nothing to be said. He cheated on her and that was the wrong move.

She heard one of the kids running to the hallway bathroom. That was her indication that someone was already up. She pulled herself out of the bed. She still was in her robe and wearing nothing, but nakedness underneath. She laughed at herself and took a hot shower.

After getting the children off to school, she returned home to find Timothy's truck in the driveway. Her heart sank. Since she wanted to cause him bodily harm, she didn't want to see him.

She pulled next to his truck. He wasn't inside. It angered her that he felt that he had the right to use his key and let himself into the house. Leaping from her car, she almost forgot to close the door before she rushed to the house. She twisted the door knob to find it unlocked. She rushed through the door.

"Hi, Vivian," Timothy said greeting her at the door.

"Why the hell are you in my house?" she asked, brushing against him.

"This is our house."

He followed her into the kitchen.

"I wouldn't come in here if I were you. What do you want?"

She glanced over at the block of knives that were within arm's reach on the countertop. She fought the urge to grab a knife and stab him in the heart repeatedly. She pressed her sweaty palms against the countertop. The thought of her three children being without both of their parents, and spending the rest of her life in prison pushed the thought out of her mind.

Timothy slowly backed out of the kitchen and stood at the entrance. The look of fear on his face let her know that he understood fully.

"I wanted to talk to you about what happened. I just need you to hear me out. That's all," he said nervously.

"I don't have anything to say to you. You should've talked long before this. It's bad enough that your drinking was tearing this marriage apart, and then to find out that you're also a liar and a cheater. It's too much for me. I didn't deserve any of this!" she yelled through tears.

"No, you don't deserve this. You were the best thing that ever happened to me. I fucked up. I know I did. I need you to give me one more chance. I can show you that I can be the man that you need me to be."

"It's a little too late for that. You didn't even feel guilty enough about your white woman to tell me before I found out! I guess you're sorry!" she spat.

"Let's not go there. Her being white had nothing to do with it."

"Black, White, or Asian, it doesn't matter! You had an affair with your boss who happens to be a white woman. How long has this been going on? You still haven't answered that question."

"I'll be honest with you. It's been about six months. I never wanted to be with her. It was a mistake. I didn't love her. You have to believe me. I'm sorry! It won't happen again. I promise. Please forgive me, Vivian. I need you to forgive me."

He clasped his hands together in a praying position.

"It will happen again. You've been lying and cheating for months! At what point was it going to end? You've already crossed the line. What is going to stop you from doing it again? Certainly not the idea of losing your family. I need you to leave!" she shouted.

Vivian leaned on the counter with her head in her hands. She kicked herself for not recognizing the signs. The drinking, keeping late hours, and the disrespect all began to make sense. The last six months of their marriage was all a lie.

"What? I don't want to go. Please don't make me go. I love you."

"If you loved me, you would've never hurt me."

"I need you. I need my family. I'm nothing without my family."

Vivian walked slowly towards Timothy and stopped in front of him. With tears in their eyes, she removed her wedding ring and placed it in his hand.

"It's over. I can't accept what you've done."

Timothy looked down at the princess cut diamond ring that he placed on her finger on their wedding day. He looked at her in disbelief, clutching the ring.

"Vivian, please. Just give us a chance."

He tried to wrap his arms around her, but she pushed away from him.

"Get out!"

"No, I love you."

He willed her to put her arms around him as he grabbed her again. Her hug was replaced with a slap across his face. He quickly grabbed her arm.

"You don't love me! If you did, you would've never hurt me like this!" she shouted.

She jerked away from him, causing him to release her. She walked over to the front door and opened it.

"Timothy, it's over," she said sternly.

"No, Vivian. I need you. I can't live without you."

"You're going to have to. You should've thought about all of that before you cheated."

"So this is it? After all these years, I fuck up one time and you want to throw it all away!" he yelled.

"No, you threw it all away when you stuck your dick in another woman!"

Timothy headed towards the door. He stopped and kissed the hand that held her ring. He placed her ring on the table. She watched him as he looked down at the ring and then back at her.

"Fuck it then Vivian! I don't need you. I came here to talk to you and apologize, but it's just not good enough for you! How in the hell are you supposed to take care of all of this? You can't do this by yourself. That little check you bring home ain't shit! You need to think about this!" he shouted.

He walked out onto the porch. She looked at him with surprise of his sudden change of attitude.

"I was waiting for the real you to show up! First, you're all sorry and apologetic. Now, you're angry and disrespectful. We will be just fine. You will be hearing from my lawyer.""That's fine. Have it your way."

He threw his hands in the air.

"I hope she finds you a damn good attorney, because you're going to need it."

She slammed the front door leaving him standing outside. A few seconds later, she heard his truck screeching out of the driveway knocking over her trash cans.

Vivian lay on the sofa in the empty and quiet house. She thought about how the children were going to feel about the divorce. What was going to be her financial situation and how was she mentally going to handle all of this? First thing's first, she needed a lawyer, and then she had to sit the children down and explain the situation when the time came. Tomorrow was the first day of a new day in their new lives.

CHAPTER 9

Vivian was still trying to digest the fact that Timothy had been unfaithful with Samantha. She and Samantha weren't the best of friends, but they had become acquainted with one another over the years. Just like any powerful and attractive woman, she kept her eye on her. Samantha was always supportive of their family. She was sure to send gifts and cards to both her and Timothy on their birthdays and anniversary.

Timothy never gave her a reason to suspect anything between them. The only time she became suspicious was when she found the birthday card Samantha had given him with hearts written all over it and saying that she loved him. Soon after, she began calling the house more frequently for Timothy, for so-called *work related issues*.

She couldn't believe he was able to carry on an affair and face her, knowing what he had done. She thought back over the past months when he had to work late or was called in unexpectedly to work. As a supportive wife, she didn't give him any grief about it. Now, she wished that she would have questioned him about his sudden change in work schedule. She hadn't and here they were.

Normally, she would have eaten breakfast, but she hadn't had an appetite. All she did was think about the pain and humiliation she felt. If she could, she would crawl under a rock. That wouldn't be possible, because she had her children to care for. She had to find her strength, which were her children. When she thought about the children, she thought about how much better off they would be with both parents, but there was no way she could accept his betrayal.

The trust she once had for him was completely gone. It was too easy for him to betray her and carry on as if he was the perfect husband and father. She felt it was nothing he could ever do to earn her trust again. She didn't have the time or patience to babysit him, worry about if he was still communicating with Samantha, or seeing her was just not in her job description. She was his wife and she didn't sign on for that.

After playing out different scenarios in her mind, she was sure that she was doing the right thing. Her mind was made up. She was moving forward with the divorce. Samantha and Timothy could have each other; they deserved each other.

Vivian didn't want to spend the remainder of her day stressing out about her situation. She needed to talk to someone, so she decided to call her mother. The house was quiet so she decided to cut on the television to kill the silence. She turned the volume down low and dialed her mother's phone number. Her dad answered on the first ring.

"Hi, dad. What are you doing?"

"Oh, hey there, baby girl. I'm just coming in from the garage. I was mounting another one of my deer heads."

"How have you been feeling?"

"I'm feeling much better than last week. This old ticker of mine gives me trouble from time to time. I'm on some new medication and I'm feeling better than ever."

She could hear shuffling around in the background. That was a good thing. There were times when he didn't have enough energy to move around the way he liked.

"I'm glad you're feeling better. You had me worried there for a minute."

"Your old man is still hanging in there. Did you call for your mother?"

"Yes, I did. I have something to tell you, too," she said nervously.

She didn't want to upset her father, but she knew he was going to find out either way.

"What's the matter, baby girl?"

She heard the seriousness in his tone.

"Timothy has been having an affair with his boss, Samantha. I'm going to file for divorce. Now, I don't want you getting upset."

"Oh, no! That damn Timothy! I told him the day you decided to marry him that if he hurt you, I was going to put a bullet in his skull. Where is my shotgun!" he shouted.

She could hear him shuffling around again.

"Dad no! There's no need to get upset now. What's done is done. He's not worth it and you know it. I will be fine if not better without him. I didn't tell you that he started drinking. We had been fighting in front of the kids, and that's not healthy for them. It's best that we go our separate ways."

"I wish you would've told me about this before. I

could've tried to talk to him about his drinking. He knew how hard it was for you growing up. Why would he do that?"

"I don't know dad. That alone was tearing our family apart. Then finding out about his affair was it."

"Well, your mother and I are here for you and our grandbabies. We support your decision. I'm going to let you talk to your mother," he said.

She heard her father sit the phone down and call out to her mother.

"Marie, pick up the phone. It's Vivian."

"Hello?"

"Hi, mom."

"George, hang up the phone. I have it," her mother called out. "Hi, honey. I was just thinking about you girl. I'm fixing your daddy a pot roast tonight, and I was going to call to see if you and the kids wanted to come over for dinner."

"Mom, I need to talk to you," she said.

Hearing her mother's voice comforted her. She wished she were right there with her to tell her what to do.

"What's wrong, baby? Is everything all right?"

"Timothy has been having an affair with his boss."

"Not Timothy. Are you sure?"

"Yes, I'm sure. I overheard them in his hotel. It was bad enough that he started drinking heavily and fighting with me in front of the children," she explained.

She could feel a lump in her throat as she listened to the disappointment in her mother's voice.

"Don't tell me it's that woman that comes to the children's birthday parties. I knew something wasn't right with her," her mother said angrily.

"Yes, that's her."

"Jesus Christ I knew it. She just didn't sit right with me from the day I first met her. I know these things you know. I tell you, women these days just don't know the hell they are going to pay in the long run for sleeping with married men. Don't get me started on the hell Timothy is going to pay!"

Vivian began to feel uneasy. Her mother did say that she felt that Samantha and Timothy were too close. She also stressed that she shouldn't be so trusting of other women around her husband.

"I'm getting a divorce."

"So your mind is made up? You're sure that you don't want to try to work it out? Divorce sounds easy, but it's really not as simple as you think. You need to be sure about this."

"I'm sure. I will never trust him again."

"Your dad hung in there with me during my addiction. I don't know where I would be if he didn't love me and was determined to save our family."

"Mom, that's different. You didn't have an affair on dad."

"I had an affair with the bottle," she said.

Things became quiet on the phone. Her mother reminded her of the lengths her father went to help her with her addiction. She realized that she just didn't have it in her and that she was definitely making the right decision.

"I'm going to come stay with you for a couple days and help with the children and around the house. This is going to be a difficult time for you and you're going to need support. No matter the outcome, you know that we are here for you. I will be there tonight," her mother said.

"Thanks, mom," she said tearfully.

"No problem, baby. I will see you later. You get some rest and quit all that worrying."

"Ok, see you."

She wiped her tears and was thankful for her parents. She no longer felt alone knowing she had their support. With her parents being older, she really didn't want to burden them. She knew that her mother and father were her biggest supporters, so she had to embrace that.

After hanging up with her mother, she wanted to get some rest. She turned off the television and headed for her bedroom. She felt a heaviness as she entered. It just didn't feel the same. She could feel Timothy's unwelcomed presence. She looked across the room at the sixteen by nineteen wedding picture in its brass custom frame. She stared at the picture shaking her head in disbelief. Marrying Timothy was one of the happiest days of her life and it showed. Her smile was radiant. She focused in on Timothy. He also appeared to be at his happiest.

The anger and hurt she felt boiled over. She ran over and pulled down their wedding picture and threw it to the floor. She stomped and kicked the picture, screaming to the top of her lungs. She didn't care who heard her. The glass was thrown all over her bedroom floor. When she was done, she looked at the damage.

The brass frame was broken on one side. The glass was broken in several places. Shards of glass hung from the frame. The glass cut the picture in several places, leaving white spots where color once shown. The picture was completely destroyed.

"I hate you! Why did you do this to me?" she screamed.

Tears continued to flow. She fell to the floor and wept. Once she was done crying, she lifted herself from the floor, cutting herself on the glass.

"Ouch! Damn it."

She examined the cut. She grabbed a napkin from the nightstand and cleaned her cut.

Her rage wasn't over yet. She stormed into the kitchen to get the trash bags. She opened the closet door and turned on the light. As she pulled and yanked every piece of clothing he had hanging down, she stuffed them into the black trash bags. She yanked on the clothes so hard, she could hear most of them tear. She stuffed his shirts, pants, jackets, and shoes in several bags. When she was done with the closet, she went over to his dresser.

In one swift movement, she swiped the contents on his dresser into an empty trash bag. One by one, she pulled out each drawer dumping the contents into more trash bags. After collecting his things, she tied up each bag. She dragged all ten bags out of the house and to the curb two at a time. Finally, she returned to her bedroom. Glass cracked under her feet, reminding her that her wedding picture was still on the floor. She picked up the broken frame with the damaged picture still inside. Carefully carrying it outside with the rest of Timothy's things, she propped the picture in front of the bags.

She pulled out her cell phone to text Timothy:

Your shit is outside. Come get it before the trash man does.

She wanted to humiliate him. He would have to load up his truck in front of the neighbors. That's if he got there before the trash man did.

CHAPTER 10

H i, honey," Leesa said.
She opened the door slowly. Leesa was Vivian's best friend. They were friends since they were ten years old. They loved each other like sisters and would do anything for each other.

Leesa was dark skinned and considered a plus sized woman. She wore her hair in long braids down her back. Her smooth dark skin was flawless and she had a beautiful smile to top it off.

"Viv, are you in here? Why is it so dark in here?" she asked.

Leesa walked over to the window, pulling back the curtains. She tripped over a pile of clothing and shoes in the middle of the floor.

"Vivian, get up!" Leesa yelled.

"Get out!" Vivian yelled from under the sheets.

"No, get up. You have been down long enough. It's time for us to have some fun. Now get your butt up!" Leesa said.

She yanked the sheets off Vivian.

"I don't feel like going anywhere," Vivian moaned.

She placed the pillow over her head.

"Don't tell me those are his pajamas? I know you're not still sleeping in his pajamas."

"No, I'm sleeping in the pajamas that I paid for."

Leesa sat on the bed next to Vivian. She rubbed her back for a few minutes as Vivian hid under her pillow.

"You have to pull yourself out of this. Life goes on after divorce. You're not going to know unless you get up from here and live. Do you think Timothy is doing the same thing you're doing? I can assure you he's not," Leesa said as honest as she could.

"I know and I have tried. I just don't want to see anyone."

"You have nothing to be ashamed of. You don't need to hide from anyone. You made your decision to divorce now stick by that."

Vivian peeked from under the pillow. She met Leesa's gaze. She knew she meant her no harm and wanted what was best for her. Leesa lifted the pillow from Vivian's head.

"How did you do it? When you divorced, it didn't seem that you went through as much as I am. It doesn't help that he constantly tells me he loves me. I know I have to move forward, but each step takes me further away from him. I vowed to walk away and never accept infidelity, but I never knew how forgiving my heart could be. Pride led me to divorce. Guilt and shame are holding me in my bed," Vivian sobbed.

"I know it hurts, but it gets better. We have plans tonight so I need you to get up and get yourself together."

Leesa got up from the bed and walked towards the door.

"I don't want to see you or anyone else!" Vivian sat up and shouted.

"Girl, now I know you gone crazy! You're not standing me up tonight! You're in bed in your ex-husband's pajamas screaming." She was laughing so hard her stomach began to hurt.

Vivian eventually joined her after realizing she was a sight for sore eyes. After the laughs, things became serious again.

"Let me get you a shower going or we will never get there on time."

Leesa went into the master bathroom and ran a hot shower for Vivian. When she returned, Vivian was sitting on the side of the bed.

"I just wanted a weekend alone. No work, no kids, and no Leesa," Vivian said jokingly.

"Too bad. I love you too much to sit back and watch you go down this lonely road. Trust me, it's a long lonely road. No one is going down there with you, especially Timothy. I moved on with my life and you will, too," Leesa said sincerely.

Tears filled Vivian's eyes as she heard the truth.

"It's not that I want his lying cheating ass. It's the betrayal."

Leesa sat next to Vivian taking her hand.

"It's always something. Now let it go. It happened and it's not a damn thing you can do about it. God is going to deal with them both. He will give you front row seats to the show."

"Amen to that!" Vivian said, managing a smile.

"I've seen it done many times before. The cheater and the mistress will get dealt with in God's time. Can't nobody do you like Jesus," Leesa said jokingly.

She raised her hands in the air.

"You got that right, girl," Vivian said giving her a high-five.

"He will make sure that you're there to see it. Trust me."

"I hope so. I will be there with popcorn."

They sat and comforted each other.

"Leesa, I never knew what you went through with your divorce."

"I wished that no one I loved ever had to feel that way."

"If I wasn't there for you, I'm sorry."

"You, my mother, and my sisters helped me more than you know. Look at me now. I'm single and independent. Most of all, I'm happy."

"I never asked, but did he cheat on you?" Vivian asked.

"No, he wasn't a cheater. He was abusive and controlling."

"I didn't know. How come you didn't say anything?"

"I hid all my bruises and emotional scars. I didn't want anyone to know that Leesa let a man make her feel less than the ground he walked on. See, I know a little bit about the pride, the guilt, and the shame that you were talking about."

"I'm so sorry, Leesa."

"Don't be sorry for me or for yourself. We both chose to put our past behind us and that's what we're supposed to be doing. We have our futures ahead of us. Now let's move forward beginning with a shower and a hot comb!" Leesa joked.

"I love you," Vivian said through tears.

"That's what friends are for."

Vivian took a hot shower and washed her hair. She washed away her depression, guilt, and shame. She said a silent prayer asking God for strength.

She stepped out of the shower to the burning smell of

her flat irons and curlers. Leesa was waiting to do her hair. She also had her outfit laid out along with her heels.

"Since you're in mourning, I figured you would want to wear black so that you can blend in with the crowd," Leesa said, picking out accessories from the jewelry box.

"How wrong you are. I want to stand out in a crowd tonight."

Vivian walked over to her walk in closet and shifted through the many dresses she had. Some still had the tags on them. She found what she was looking for. She pulled out a cream bandage dress.

"Now that's more like it," Leesa said with a snap.

She gave her a nod of approval.

"I know right. This is the dress!"

Vivian placed the dress against her body and modeled in the mirror.

"Girl, you still got it going on. Now come on, because we have reservations."

"Where are we going anyway?"

"You shall see. I promise you that you're going to enjoy yourself tonight." She walked over and took Vivian's hands into hers.

"No surprises and no blind dates!"

"I just want to take you out to get some air. It'll be fun."

"Well, can I get dressed in private?" Vivian asked jokingly.

Leesa took Vivian to a nice restaurant and lounge called *The Shore*. Vivian and Leesa enjoyed fresh seafood and cocktails. At the end of the night, Vivian was thankful that her friend pulled her out of the bed. Vivian was ready for the next phase of her life.

CHAPTER 11

Vivian waited three months before telling the children about the pending divorce. During that time, Timothy visited the children twice a month. After receiving the divorce papers, he visited them once a month.

The past three months were a struggle for Vivian. She was still dealing with heartache, stress, and depression. Her life changed overnight. Increased headaches plagued her constantly. She fought with her decision to end her marriage without trying to work it out. Due to the lack of sleep and skipped meals, she lost ten pounds from her already petite frame. She felt as if she was in a whirlwind.

She decided to sit down one Saturday afternoon to discuss the divorce with her children. She called them to the living room. Dominic, Demetrius, and Journey joined her on the sofa.

"I have something to tell you guys."

The children looked at her with concern except Journey.

She was smiling from ear to ear. She always anticipated good news.

"You know that daddy lives in Charlotte for work now, right?"

They all nodded their heads. Journey still smiling.

"Well, mommy and daddy aren't going to be able to live together anymore. We are not moving to Charlotte and daddy isn't coming back to live with us. We are still your mother and father, and nothing is ever going to change that. Your dad will try to visit you as much as he can. Do you understand?"

"Does that mean you're getting a divorce?" Dominic asked.

"Yes, we are getting a divorce. No matter what happens, it doesn't change how much we love you. We are still going to be a family, because we have you."

"Are we still going to see daddy sometimes?" Demetrius asked.

"Of course... He plans to visit as much as he can and you can call him every day if you want to."

"Okay," Demetrius said with a smile.

"Journey, do you understand?" she asked.

"Yes. I understand, but I still love daddy," Journey said.

"I know you still love your daddy. He loves you, too. You can call him anytime you want. Nothing is going to change that," she explained.

"I love you, too, mommy," Journey said.

"I love you, too. Hugs everybody!" she said.

They all embraced one another.

Vivian felt a little better about her decision to move forward with the divorce. The children's reaction worried her, but now she saw just how strong and understanding her children were. It was going to be very important for

Timothy to speak with them on a regular basis as well as visit as often as possible.

During the next ten months, Timothy continued to pay the bills. Financially, things were still tight, but the bills were getting paid. Timothy attempted to salvage his marriage by continually asking her for forgiveness. When he came to visit the children, he would ask for sex. Vivian turned him down every time. The more she tried to push him away, the more she realized that they still had to have some sort of relationship with each other for the children's sake and business matters. As time came to an end, so did his visits and financial help.

CHAPTER 12

After a long day of work and two interviews, Vivian was exhausted. The kids were still adjusting to their father's absence. The twins were fighting more than usual, and Dominic stayed in his room all day playing video games ignoring everyone in the house.

Vivian kicked off her heels and removed her pantyhose letting out a sigh of relief. She gave the children their instructions and proceeded to prepare dinner.

After getting the children all settled in after fighting with Demetrius to turn off the television, she finally had time for herself. These were the days when she missed having a husband around. She and Timothy would split the responsibilities around the house. Usually, he cleaned the kitchen after dinner and read books to the kids. Now, Vivian had to cook, clean, bathe the children, and put them to bed. She made it all happen even if she was a tired mess by the time she made it to bed.

Vivian stretched out in bed flailing her arms and legs as if she were making a snow angel. She appreciated and enjoyed having a bed to herself. She could stretch from one end to the next and wrap the sheets around her body without a complaining party. Most of all, she had more closet space. She had room for all of the shoes she owned, and she could finally organize her closet exactly the way she wanted it.

There was one downside to not having a man, sex. It seemed like forever since she had sex. It had been fourteen months to be exact. She'd recently settled for sex toys for the time being. Vivian reached into her nightstand and felt for the purple velvet bag that was pushed to the back that held *pleasure*. After three days of online shopping for a suitable replacement for a penis, she settled on a vibrator that she thought would do the job and it did.

Vivian reached under the sheets sliding her hands down pass her erect nipples and cupped her breast. She gently squeezed them with her eyes closed and pressed her hips deep into the pillowtop mattress. She ran her hands up and down her thighs spreading them apart as she moaned in anticipation of *pleasure*.

Finally, finding her way to her center, she rubbed gently. Pleasure ran down her toes sending electrifying sensations. She penetrated herself using long strokes at first and then shorter faster strokes as she reached an orgasm.

The only thing that is missing is a warm body against mine. Lord, I know I need to use this time to find myself, but I need a man.

Vivian's alarm sounded off and ringing filled her bedroom. She was already awake. Last night sleep didn't come easy as she lay in bed anticipating her meeting the next morning. She looked over at the twelve month nature calendar hanging on her wall. The month of December was represented by snowcapped mountains. December 9th was circled in red ink over and over. Today was the day that she would sign the final draft of the property settlement agreement. After some negotiation, they were able to come to an agreement. She pulled herself out of the bed and prepared herself for the meeting.

Vivian and Timothy sat across from each other alongside their attorneys. Timothy was dressed in his Sunday's best and Vivian wore a classy fitted suit and button down blouse.

Vivian's cousin Lynda was her attorney. She was more than happy to assist her in her divorce, pro bono. Timothy's attorney was bought and paid for by Samantha.

The meeting was brief, but final. They came to an agreement on custody. Vivian received sole custody while allowing Timothy visitation. She was granted the house and child support was ordered as well as alimony. All together granting her a total of thirteen hundred dollars a month.

She hated Timothy even more, because he knew with the alimony and child support she could barely cover the mortgage payments. Outside of their legal agreements, he promised that he would help her as much as he could until she found a new job. Vivian knew that wouldn't last long, and she refused to beg him for money every month.

She had interviews lined up and worked as many hours as she could to pay her bills. All she needed was a few months to land a job. She knew she could find something in her profession, but with the job market, it was going to be hard.

"Is that all?" Vivian asked Lynda, after signing all of the paperwork that was handed to her. She intentionally tried to avoid any physical or eye contact with Timothy. It was hard enough going through with the divorce.

"I think we are just about done," Lynda responded.

She gave Vivian a smile to let her know that everything was going as planned.

"I have something for you and the kids," Timothy finally said.

He slipped his hand into his suit pocket and pulled out a check. He slid the check across the table to Vivian.

"What is this?" she asked.

"Your share of the stocks I owned." They both stared at each other for a moment.

"Thank you. We are done here," Lynda said.

She began to shake hands as she claimed victory.

Vivian picked up the check. It was for ten thousand dollars. Only God knew how bad she needed that money. Her eyes watered. Everyone stood to conclude the meeting. Timothy walked around the table to Vivian. She stood and reached her hand out for him to shake. It was clear that he wanted a hug, but she couldn't. Usually, her heart melted at his bedroom eyes. Instead, they made her sick to her stomach.

"Timothy."

Her hand was still out there for him to shake.

Reluctantly, he shook her hand.

"I'm so sorry. I never meant to hurt you."

"I'm sure you didn't mean to destroy our family. You meant to get away with it," she said sarcastically.

She met his gaze, yanking her hand from his. That was the encounter she tried to avoid. She didn't have any more room for *sorry*. Her cup was full.

"Please believe me when I say that I'm sorry. I will always love you, Vivian."

"Well, I won't love you. Your kids will always be yours, but I'm not."

She walked out.

Lynda rushed to catch up to Vivian with her briefcase and papers in hand. Vivian's heels hit the marble floors with force. She was now a single mother who was once sheltered in a marriage. The finality of the divorce hit her like a ton of bricks. She couldn't hold in her emotions any longer. She grabbed her stomach and mouth as a cry left her body. She rushed into a nearby restroom almost knocking over a woman that was leaving. She walked to the nearest sink and looked at herself in the mirror. She felt sick. She turned on the cold water and splashed her face.

She pushed open a stall door just when her breakfast decided to make an appearance. She fell to her knees and cried for her children, Timothy, and the family she once had.

If it weren't for the fresh roll of toilet paper, she would've had to face the onlookers with a mess on her face.

She could hear someone asking if she was all right, and they were even bold enough to try to push the door open. Vivian quickly slammed it shut. She wiped her mouth and face the best she could before facing the strangers.

This was your decision. You made the right decision.

She stood to her feet and noticed that her skirt fell victim to her mess. She wiped her skirt the best she could, but it was ruined.

"Vivian, are you all right?" Lynda asked from the other side of the door.

"I'll be out," Vivian called out.

She was so embarrassed.

She opened the door expecting to see women looking

at her with pity. Instead, she found Lynda.

"Where did everyone go?" Vivian asked.

"I told them to mind their own damn business. Are you okay?"

"I guess. When the day came, I didn't think it would be this hard. I'll be fine," Vivian said letting out a deep breath. "I know I did the right thing. Right?"

"Vivian it's never easy when you love someone, especially when you're forced to make that final decision. You did what you felt was best for you. It doesn't matter what I think or anyone else," Lynda said. "Besides, you can always do it all over again if you change your mind."

"I'll pass. Did you see him in there in his fancy suit and cuff links? I'm sure Ms. Bourgeois dressed him."

"I knew you were going to say something about that. All I knew was that she had better not showed her face in there."

They both laughed.

"Thanks for everything Lynda."

"That's what family is for. Now look at you. Clean yourself up and let's celebrate!" Lynda said.

They embraced each other.

Vivian wasn't really up for a celebration. Her marriage had come to an end and her life as well as her children's was going to be very different. She wasn't sure what her future held, but she had to go and find out.

Walking out of the building and into a new life gave her butterflies. She thought her stomach would betray her once again when she saw Timothy getting into a car with Samantha. She thought he was already gone, and she didn't expect to have to see the two of them together.

For most of the drive, Vivian sat quietly. She thought about how long it had been since she dated.

She said aloud, "I am officially DIVORCED!"

CHAPTER 13

Vivian pulled into the closest parking space to Leesa's townhome. Leesa was celebrating her thirty-sixth birthday with a dinner party. It was 8:30 p.m. and the parking lot was almost full. She turned off the engine and headlights. Flipping down the visor, she checked her makeup. While retrieving her makeup bag, she heard someone walking up to the car. She looked up to find Leesa smiling at the passenger door trying to open it. Vivian unlocked the door.

"What are you doing?" Vivian asked.

"I need to talk to you," Leesa said.

She slid into the passenger's seat. Her perfume, *DOT* by Marc Jacobs filled the car.

"You look gorgeous!" Vivian said.

Vivian was stunned by Leesa's appearance. They went shopping earlier in the week for her birthday dress. She'd seen the dress without it being on Leesa. The dress didn't make Leesa, Leesa made the dress. She wore a sleeveless black and silver metallic party dress with a sweetheart neckline by Adrianna Papell. The black and silver sling back Nine West pumps completed the look.

"Thank you," she said in a sassy tone.

"What's wrong? What do you need to talk to me about?" Vivian asked while retrieving her New York apple red lipstick from her makeup bag. She began to add a fresh coat. She pretended not to hear Leesa as she put on her makeup.

"I have someone I want you to meet tonight. His name is James." She waited for a response. "Did you hear me?"

Vivian's face turned red. She finished her makeup by applying a touch of eyeliner. She closed the visor after one last look.

"I'm here to celebrate your birthday and you're playing matchmaker? Please don't try to hook me up."

"I've already told him about you and he wants to meet you. Just be nice okay?" Leesa said.

She opened the door, exited the car, and then said, "Come on girl."

"Do you have any gloss?" Leesa asked as they walked to the door.

"Yeah, I have a shimmering pink gloss that would look nice on you," she said dryly.

She reached into her purse and handed the lip gloss to Leesa.

Leesa's mother, Janice opened the door just as they approached.

"I was wondering what was taking you two so long," she said in a southern drawl.

"I was telling her that we have someone for her to meet and to be nice," Leesa said.

She gave Vivian a wink.

"Hi, Janice," Vivian said, shaking her head.

She gave her a friendly hug and went into the house followed by Leesa.

Inside, Leesa had transformed her townhome into an inviting setting. Vivian could tell that she moved some of her furniture out of the living room. There was an open space in the middle of the living room floor for dancing. She couldn't miss the abundance of silver and black balloons and streamers throughout. The music played nicely in the background; not too loud. A couple sat on the sofa with champagne in hand. There were others standing around talking.

Leesa took Vivian by the hand and began to introduce her to everyone. Some of the guests were new faces. She knew Leesa's three sisters, mother, and father. She greeted each one of them with hugs and kisses. She was introduced to the other guests.

"James, this is my friend Vivian. Vivian, this is James," Leesa said.

She stepped back allowing them to greet each other.

"Hi. It's nice to meet you," Vivian said, extending her hand.

"It's nice to meet you," he said.

He took her hand in his, brought it to his lips, and placed two soft kisses on it. Vivian smiled and slowly lowered her hand. She could feel the heat in her face and knew she was turning red.

"Can I get you a glass of champagne?" he asked.

"Yes, thanks," she said. Her cheeks turned red.

Vivian felt like a little school girl. James was handsome. He was short in stature but charming. He wore neat dreadlocks pulled back into a ponytail. When James walked away, Leesa pulled her to the side.

"So, what do you think? He's cute right?"

"He is cute. Not quite my type, but he's interesting," Vivian admitted.

"You ladies aren't talking about me are you?" James asked, as he approached the two of them.

He handed both Vivian and Leesa a glass of champagne.

"Thank you," they both said.

Vivian took a sip from her glass.

"Well, I have other guests to entertain. I will leave you two to entertain each other," Leesa said jokingly.

James and Vivian smiled at Leesa. Vivian walked over to a nearby chair and invited James to join her.

"So, what do you do for a living?" Vivian asked.

"I'm a chiropractor. I'm moving to Atlanta to start my own practice next month, which I'm looking forward to."

"A chiropractor? I didn't take you for the doctor type."

"I get that all the time. It goes to prove that you can't judge a book by its cover. And you?"

"Well, I have a degree in human resource management, but I'm working part time right now," she said.

She didn't want him to ask where so she moved the conversation along.

"Leesa really did her thing this year. I can't wait to see what's for dinner. It smells great," she said, looking around the room.

Leesa stood in the middle of the room ringing a bell. The music lowered and she had everyone's attention.

"Dinner is served. Everyone, please head over to the dining area," she said, pointing in the direction of the dining room.

The small crowd of guests followed Leesa. Before they were able to make it into the dining room, could hear the guests gasp. Vivian quickly made her way into the dining room to see what the big deal was. There was a table prepared for a castle. There were steaks, lobsters, and cocktail shrimp at each table setting. There was also a spread of vegetables and buttered rolls.

"Leesa, you have really outdone yourself!" Vivian yelled over the crowd.

"Thanks, but I can't take all of the credit. My mother was a huge help."

She turned towards her mother and blew her a kiss.

Everyone found a seat around the table and Leesa said grace. Leesa sat at the head of the table and Vivian sat to her right. James sat directly across from Vivian. The food was awesome. Towards the end of dinner, Janice offered a toast to Leesa.

"To a fabulous woman who has brought nothing, but happiness in my life. You have accomplished great things. You're a phenomenal woman. I love you and I wish you a happy birthday."

"Thank you and I love you, too," Leesa said, almost in tears.

Glasses clinked and everyone said happy birthday to Leesa in unison. Her mother came out with a three tiered custom designed cake. It was white icing, draped in black and silver ribbon, cascading down the side of the cake. On top was a black platform pump with silver studs on the back of the heel all done in fondant. Everyone applauded.

After cake, the guests began to leave one by one. Vivian and James hadn't talked since before dinner. Leesa and Vivian sat on the sofa admiring the black diamond earrings and necklace set her parents presented to her. They were beautiful.

"Ladies, can I join you?" James asked.

He handed Vivian another glass of champagne.

"Thanks, but I think I've had enough," she said politely.

She sat the glass down on the table.

"Sure, you can join us," Leesa said.

James took a seat beside Vivian. He sat close enough to rub his leg against her leg.

"I thought you left. I haven't seen you," Vivian said.

"No, not without seeing you first. I was thinking that we could get together one day for lunch or maybe dinner," he said.

"Yes, she would love to go," Leesa said for her.

Vivian elbowed her in her side. Leesa fell over in laughter.

"Damn, Viv I was just playing!"

"Sure, I would like that," she said for herself.

James playfully wiped sweat from his forehead.

"I thought you were going to shoot me down."

He lifted his glass for a toast.

"No. I would, but I've had enough to drink," Vivian said.

"Come on Vivian, join me," he said, as he held his glass in the air.

Vivian reluctantly retrieved the glass of champagne from the table and toasted. After she had finished the glass of champagne, she began to feel lightheaded. Thinking that she had reached her limit, she decided to call it a night. She went over to Leesa to let her know that she was leaving. She remembered Leesa asking James to see her out to her car. That was the last thing she remembered of that night.

CHAPTER 14

The next morning, Vivian was awakened by her mother. Vivian was supposed to get the children hours earlier. When her mother didn't see or hear from her, she decided to check on her.

"Wake up, wake up!" Vivian's mother yelled.

Vivian slowly began to come to. Her eyelids fluttered a few times before she was able to open them. Her head ached and her vision was blurry.

"Mom, is that you?" she asked.

"Thank you, Jesus! I thought you were dead! What happened to you?" her mother asked.

Her mother was clutching her heart and almost in tears.

"I don't know," she said.

Vivian sat up slowly.

"What happened to you? You slept half the day away and didn't call once to check on your children. Did you have too much to drink at that party?"

"I honestly don't remember. I don't know what happened."

"Let me get you some coffee. You just sit here. I will be right back."

Vivian was very confused. She searched through her clouded mind for memories of the night before. They came in flashes. She tried to remember the drive home, but couldn't. There were no memories of her coming home or going to bed. She fought hard to conjure those memories up, but failed.

She looked down and realized she was naked. She was laying on top of her sheets. She quickly pulled the covers over her body.

"What in the hell!" she shouted.

She did not remember undressing or how she got home. She frantically searched the floor for her clothing. She didn't see them.

"Mom!" she shouted.

She placed her feet on the floor and stood slowly. That was when she felt throbbing between her legs. She reached down and felt wetness. She ran to the bathroom.

"What's the matter?" her mother asked, running into the room.

"I think something happened!"

"What happened, baby? What's wrong?"

She found Vivian in the bathroom moving around frantically.

"Calm down, baby and talk to me."

She grabbed Vivian and stood in front of her.

"Look at me. Look at me now. What's wrong?"

Vivian looked her mother in the eyes.

"I think that I had sex, but I don't remember. It feels like I did, but I'm not sure."

"Tell me what happened last night. Did you leave the party with someone? Did anyone follow you home?"

"Mom, I don't remember. I'm trying to remember last night and I can't. It's like I lost my memory."

Her mother led her back into her bedroom and sat her on the bed. Vivian was frantic and in tears.

"You need to calm down and think real hard. What is the last thing you remember?"

Vivian slowed her breathing and closed her eyes. She fought through her cloudy mind once again. Her mother sat patiently.

"I remember feeling sick before I left. I met a guy at Leesa's party. He gave me the last drink I had."

"He probably put something in your drink. That's why you can't remember anything. I'm going to call the police and report this."

"No, mom! I don't even know what happened. I could be wrong," she said.

"And you could be right. We have to call for help. They have doctors that can figure it out for you."

"No! Please don't call!" she pleaded, grabbing her arm.

"Vivian, why don't you want me to call?" her mother asked as she looked into her eyes.

"Please, mom. I don't know what happened. I might've had too much to drink. That's all," she said.

She wanted and needed her mother to believe her. She was terrified at the thought that she was sexually assaulted by someone and didn't know it.

"Are you sure? If something did happen, you and the police need to know. You don't know what these men have out here. What if he does the same thing to someone else?"

"Mom, I'm sure I had too much to drink. I'm just freaking out," she lied to her mother.

Her mother narrowed her eyes and peered directly into them knowing she wasn't truthful.

"Well, if you say so. If you're all right, I have to get back to the house. I can keep the kids as long as you need. Make sure you call me," her mother said apprehensively.

"I will be fine mom. I will get the kids in a few hours."

She could tell that her mother was concerned. Her mother kept pulling at her, something she did when she was worried.

"Vivian, when things like this happen, it's never the woman's fault. There's nothing for you to be ashamed of."

"Mom, I was wrong. I had too much to drink that's all. I'm so glad you came to check on me, thanks."

She gave her mom a long tight hug.

Her mother walked to her car, but stopped to look back at Vivian. She gave her mother a reassuring look. She did all of this with one quick nod and a strained smile. All the while, she was falling apart on the inside.

CHAPTER 15

Vivian debated on whether or not she should bathe. She figured that the doctor would need to collect samples for evidence. She felt dirty and wanted to wash away any traces of the night before.

Calling the police crossed her mind, but she wasn't sure what happened and wasn't sure what she would say. It wasn't clear if she was drunk and invited James back to her house for sex. That was completely out of her character. She gave herself a headache trying to remember what happened. She knew she had to do something and fast.

"Hello, Dr. Jones' office," a young a woman answered.

"Hi, I'm a patient of Dr. Jones and I really need to see her today," Vivian said calmly.

"May I have your name and date of birth?"

Vivian released the information to the young woman on the other end of the phone. Dreading her next question, she sighed heavily.

"What do you need to be seen for?"

"I'm having a female issue that I need to discuss with her. Are there any appointments today?"

"She can see you today at four o'clock or nine tomorrow morning."

"I'll take the four o'clock."

Vivian wanted to call James and ask what happened, but she didn't remember if he had given her his number. She noticed her trembling hands as she dialed Leesa's number. She squeezed her hands together to calm her nerves.

"Hey, girl," Leesa said cheerfully.

"Hey. How was your party? Sorry, I left early."

Vivian tried to put some excitement in her voice.

"It was great. It ended about an hour after you left. How was your night?"

There was silence for a few moments.

"That's why I was calling. Was I drunk last night? How did I get home?"

"You were a little tipsy. That's why you left early. James offered to drive you home in your car and catch a cab back to his place since he didn't live far from you. Don't you remember?"

"To answer your question, no I don't remember. I woke up and my mom was standing over me. I was in bed naked and couldn't remember how I got there."

There was a brief silence.

"What are you saying?"

"I think he raped me."

Vivian whispered those words as if she didn't want anyone else to hear their conversation.

"Where are you? Are you okay?"

"I'm at home, but I'm about to go to my doctor's appointment. I'm fine, I think."

"Did you call the police yet?"

"What am I going to say? I was at a party and I was drinking. Then I was flirting with a man that I think raped me. Leesa, I don't remember what happened. I could've been so drunk that I willingly had sex with him."

"Have you talked to him? He is the only one that knows what happened."

"No, I don't have his number. The last thing I remember was telling you I was leaving."

"It sounds like he could've put something in your drink. He did hand you a few drinks last night. I'm on my way over there. I'm going to call him and see what he has to say. Vivian, I'm so sorry this happened to you. If I thought something like this would have happened, I would have never trusted him to drive you home."

"I know. It's not your fault. It just seems like my life is a train wreck. I just don't know anymore."

"It's going to be all right. I'm on my way. I love you, girl."

"See you and I love you, too."

After hanging up with Leesa, Vivian rushed into the bathroom. She lost it right there on the toilet. She felt overwhelmed with emotion. Men were hurting her at each corner she turned. First, Timothy and now a man she shared a few hours with. He even found a way to violate her. She knew she wasn't a bad person. All of her life, she'd been the nice, respectful young woman. She was a faithful wife and devoted mother. She failed to make sense of it all.

After pulling herself together, she ran a hot bath. Steam rose as the bubbles formed and filled the tub. She first dipped her toes into the hot water to test the temperature. It stung, but she slowly emerged the rest of her body into the steamy hot water. When her body was used to the heat, she was able to relax. She slid her body deeper into the water until she could rest her head comfortably on the back of the tub. She closed her eyes and cried. Her tears fell down her cheeks and into the water. She soaked in the tub and then proceeded to scrub her skin until it burned. She washed herself over and over again.

Vivian dressed in a comfortable gray jogging suit. She applied mousse on her hair and wore it curly. She didn't have much of an appetite, but her stomach rumbled. She decided to eat a packet of instant oatmeal and glass of orange juice.

The doorbell rang before she could finish her meal.

"Who is it?" Vivian called out.

"It's me. Open up!" Leesa yelled through the door.

Vivian opened the door slowly. Leesa walked in cautiously.

"Hi, honey," Leesa said, hugging Vivian tightly.

"Hey, I'm fine."

Vivian pulled back from her.

"What time is your appointment? I'm driving you."

"It's at four."

"I called James."

Vivian's stomach flipped at the mention of his name. Leesa followed Vivian back to the kitchen. She sat at the table to finish her food.

"So, what did he say?" Vivian asked nervously.

She poked at her oatmeal with a spoon. Leesa took a seat across from her.

"This fool had the nerve to say he didn't touch you. After some not so kind words and the threat of calling the police, he finally started talking. He claimed that he drove you home and you willingly had sex with him. He said you were well aware of what was happening. He said he didn't want to tell me your business, because if you wanted me to know, then you would have told me yourself."

"You know I'm not that person. I can't remember what happened, but I know I didn't have sex willingly. He had to have put something in my drink."

"What do you want to do? You can make a police report and let them sort it out. Did you shower?"

"Yes, I did."

"Why did you do that? You just washed away the evidence!"

Leesa angrily smacked her hand on the kitchen table.

"I had to wash his filth off of me! I couldn't..." She broke down again.

"Oh, I'm sorry for upsetting you. I just don't want him to get away with this. I feel somewhat responsible for what happened."

Leesa slid her chair over to Vivian and put her arms around her. She rubbed her back.

"Stop saying that. It's not your fault."

"Ok, girl lets go. I don't want you to be late for your appointment. I will support any decision you decide to make."

Leesa reached into her purse and pulled out a yellow post it. She handed it to Vivian.

"What is this?" Vivian asked.

"All the information you need on James in case you decided to press charges on him. Or if you want me to call up my cousins to handle this," Leesa said jokingly.

Vivian laughed and finally smiled.

She felt somewhat happier. Although, she didn't accept the offer, she pondered it. Leesa drove Vivian to her appointment. Vivian requested an STD screening, which Dr. Jones performed with no questions asked. She didn't disclose the reason for her request, but shared that she and Timothy were no longer together.

CHAPTER 16

A fter deciding not to press charges against James, she realized she needed to see a psychiatrist about what happened. She found herself unable to trust men and she knew that would interfere with her ever being in a relationship. She thanked God every day for a clean bill of health after the encounter with James.

Vivian sat in front of her computer and logged onto the website to make her mortgage payment. It was a struggle making the payments every month. Deciding between paying the utilities, food on the table, or the roof over their heads became a constant worry. Although, she received ten thousand dollars from Timothy, the money went fast.

She moved the mouse around debating on whether or not she should click the submit button. There was the past due electric bill and she needed groceries. She sighed and clicked away. Her life revolved around interviews, home, and the electronic store.

She took a full time shift at the store during the week. She also took the occasional weekend shift to make extra money. She had sixteen hundred dollars in the bank after making her mortgage payment. After each mortgage payment, her bank account dwindled.

It was long overdue for her to get back into her profession. Vivian was trying her hardest to land a job. She applied for every job that came open in the human resources field. After all the applications, both online and in person, she managed to snag a few interviews.

"It won't be long before we're in the poor house," she mumbled from her kitchen table. She was startled by a knock on the door. It was Leesa.

"Girl, I just had a date with a doctor I met online. Let me rephrase that, he's a surgeon!" she said.

Leesa sashayed into the house.

"Can those leather pants get any tighter?"

She watched her friend float around the room.

"Did I say he was absolutely gorgeous?"

"Where online did you say you met him? You have to be careful these days meeting people off the internet."

Leesa finally took a seat. Vivian went to the kitchen to get a bottle of Moscato and two wine glasses.

"It wasn't just any dating site. All of the men on the site must go through a screening process before joining the site to make sure they're not a pervert or anything like that."

"Who is he and how did the date go? I can see he has you floating on cloud nine."

She poured two glasses of wine and handed one to Leesa.

"He was sharp. You know I love a man that can dress. He's bald, chocolate, and sexy. Just the way I like it. He was very professional and respectful during the entire date. He had a great sense of humor and was the perfect gentleman. I felt like a queen all night!"

"That's how a man is supposed to make a woman feel."

"He asked me out on a second date, but I told him I would let him know."

"Okay, he is handsome, respectful, and the perfect gentleman and you turned him down? I don't get that."

"I know that you've been out of the game a while, but you can't be easy. Men like to chase."

"Oh, I guess you're right."

"I think you should try it. Just use the fourteen day trial. If you like it, just pay the monthly fee. Just let someone know where you're going and with whom. Where is your computer?" Leesa asked.

She spotted the laptop on the kitchen table. After walking to the table, she opened it.

"I'm not meeting a stranger online! You have to be crazy if you think I'm doing that!"

Vivian walked over to the table and noticed Leesa was already on the dating site.

"You don't have to meet anyone in person. Even if you just want to talk to a man. Every woman needs companionship."

She continued to type away.

"I don't know about this. I already have these Facebook stalkers. Ever since I changed my status from married to single men have been sending me all types of messages. Let's not even talk about the pictures."

"Just give it a try. If you find someone you like, I suggest you Skype first. Some of the men are using their high school photos and have gained weight and lost hair since then."

"See, that's what I'm talking about. You don't know who these men are."

Vivian watched Leesa build her profile. She opposed the entire idea, but didn't do anything to stop her. In a sense, she was curious to see if she could find someone she would like. On the other hand, the risk of meeting someone crazy made her very apprehensive. The thought of running across a psycho frightened her.

"Girl, what if I run across a crazy man stalking women online or something."

"I'm not saying that there aren't crazies out there, but you might meet husband number two. You'll never know."

"I don't know about this."

"It's time for you to start dating. Timothy is laid up with the boss lady and you're a hermit."

Leesa slid the computer over to Vivian.

Vivian wasn't sure if this was something that she wanted to do. She was ready to move on. She wanted to tell Leesa how Timothy had become an alcoholic. The last she heard, he had lost his job and was helping his uncle at his garage.

"Timothy doesn't even call his kids anymore," Vivian said over her shoulders.

"I would have never thought he would treat you and the kids that way."

Vivian completed her profile information. She was still a bit nervous about the idea of internet dating. She looked over her profile and began answering the questions.

"I hope I don't sound boring. All I do now is work and take care of my children. Leesa, make sure I sound interesting. You're the one with all of the experience," Vivian joked.

Leesa poured the last of the Moscato into her wine glass. She looked over Vivian's shoulder at the answers she provided.

"Oh, make sure you put on some makeup and take a fresh picture to post on the site. Don't be scared to be a little sexy, Viv. A little bit of cleavage wouldn't hurt," Leesa said, laughing although serious.

"Bye girl. You take it easy on the doctor now."

They kissed each other on the cheek.

Vivian watched Leesa until she got to her car. She was happy and it showed. She thought about the possibility of finding someone that could put a smile on her face.

Vivian returned to her computer. She browsed through her picture folder in search of that sexy picture she needed to put on her profile. There were only family photos. Looking at the pictures of the happy times she and Timothy shared with their family, brought tears to her eyes. She was truly a happy wife at one time.

After making up her face and putting on the sexiest top she could find, she snapped pictures of herself. After several photos, she posted them on the dating site. She was excited so she called Leesa.

"I did it!" Vivian screamed into the phone.

"Did what?" Leesa asked puzzled.

"I actually finished my profile on that dating site. I took a photo and posted my profile picture," Vivian said excitingly.

"Good for you, Viv. I knew that if I didn't set up that account, you wouldn't have gone through with it. Don't meet anyone unless it is in a public place. Also, make sure you let me or someone else know if you plan on meeting someone," Leesa said cautiously.

"Is there anything else you forgot to tell me?"

Vivian slouched down in her seat with regret.

"Some men are too busy for relationships and are just looking for a friend. You know there are men who just want sex. So don't take them all so seriously. Just have fun, but if you do meet someone you like, just make sure that you're ready."

"It would be nice to find a *Big Poppa* to wine and dine me. *Big Poppa* can help pay some of these bills around here," Vivian said jokingly.

"As long as he isn't married."

"Of course not! I would never date a married man. I'm not even looking for a relationship right now. I just want to date," Vivian shrieked.

"I hear you. We both are on the same page. I'm having the time of my life with no strings attached," Leesa emphasized.

They both shared a laugh.

"I will let you know how it goes."

"Yes, you do that."

They hung up. Vivian returned to her computer. She took in a deep breath.

"Here goes nothing."

After completing her profile, she became more optimistic about dating. Doc had Leesa on cloud nine and she wanted the same thing. She was still young and had a lot to offer in a relationship. The dating site was just the first step in moving forward and meeting new people.

CHAPTER 17

Vivian's week was filled with interviews and long, exhausting work hours. This week was unusually long with all the interviews she had. It was Friday and she'd had four interviews that week and not one job offer.

All she needed was a decent salary to take care of her family. Vivian had a degree and a few years work experience in the field, but it wasn't enough. The unemployment rate was at an all-time high and people were fighting for the same jobs. She even let go of her long ponytail and went for a more professional look. She cut her hair and went short and sleek.

Vivian decided to check her email for interview responses she might have missed. While cleaning out her inbox, she saw an email from the dating site she registered with. It had been a week since she signed up.

"Oh, my God," she murmured under her breath.

She nervously clicked on the email. She became excited and unconsciously rubbed her thighs together. The thought of being one step closer to having a man in her life aroused her. The email stated that she had a message and to log into her account. She clicked on the link.

"Ok, let's see what we have here."

She typed away at the keys quickly. She logged into the site.

There was a message waiting to be read. She clicked on the first message. A photo popped up on the screen along with a profile. She was taken aback by the photo. His screen name was *RealLeo46*.

"Really? Is this the best that I can do these days?" Vivian asked herself.

The only thing that could be said about *RealLeo46* was that he had perfectly white teeth. He went for a more 1970's look with an S-curl. It appeared that he wore makeup to cover the acne scars on his face, because he appeared pale in his photo. The jury was out on the rest. She read the brief message aloud.

"Hello my Queen, I found that we both share a lot of the same interest and both newly divorced. I must say, you're absolutely gorgeous. Let's talk," she said sarcastically.

She stared at the screen feeling unfulfilled, but she was still curious about *RealLeo46*.

She hit the chat button and a window popped up on the right side of the screen indicating that he was already online. He was definitely ready to talk. He sent a message immediately once seeing that Vivian was also online.

She slowly hit the reply button after typing, *Hello*.

She hit the send button.

Immediately he typed, *How are you SexiAries35?*

A smile crept across Vivian's face as her guard was slowly letting down just enough to enjoy the chat session. They chatted about their apprehensions to online dating and dating experiences. He had a great sense of humor and made her laugh. Vivian began to see past his looks. She became comfortable enough to reveal her first name and so did he. His name was Leon. She laughed at all of his jokes until her cheeks hurt. After their chat, she agreed to meet him at a nearby Starbucks the next day.

Vivian arrived at Starbucks fifteen minutes early. There were a few empty tables available. The line was long as usual with people impatiently waiting to place their orders. She made her way to a clean empty table by the window. Her plan was to see if she could stomach seeing him in person. His personality seemed to overshadow the unattractiveness.

I hope like hell he takes bad photos.

She watched the crowd closely looking for Leon.

"Vivian?" a voice said from behind her, startling her.

"Huh?" Vivian asked, quickly turning around.

"I thought that was you. How are you?" a very polite Leon asked. He extended his hand.

Vivian's voice was stuck in her throat. She stared at him as if she saw a ghost. She didn't move.

"I'm sorry if I startled you. I decided to come early and get us a table. Great minds do think alike."

He took a seat without Vivian offering.

"Oh, I'm so sorry. I didn't expect you to be here," she said politely.

She remembered that she didn't shake his hand. She extended her hand across the table and he accepted.

Vivian couldn't help but notice his teeth. Either his family came from a long line of perfect teeth or he paid a small fortune for his beauties. His skin was plagued by old acne scars that showed through his cocoa skin. His hands were extremely soft and manicured with a coat of clear polish. He wore a white polo shirt and black slacks. He had rings on almost every finger and two small gold rope chains around his neck. No one could miss the diamond accented watch he wore. It was a bit much for Vivian's taste.

They placed their orders and made small talk while waiting.

"What did you say you did for a living?" she asked.

"I'm a defense attorney. I also own a few real estate properties."

"That's great. I'm sure it's a very demanding job." Vivian quickly sipped her latte.

"I work this hard so that I can provide for my queen."

"One day I hope you will meet that queen who will appreciate all your hard work," she said nervously.

Leon reached across the table for Vivian's hand. She kept them on her lap. When he realized that she wasn't going to oblige him, he sat back in his chair.

"Is everything okay?" he asked.

"Yes, I'm fine. I just don't think it's appropriate for us to be holding hands in public," she said as politely as she could.

Leon reached into his back pocket and slid an envelope across the table.

"I just wanted to give you something. I know that I'm not the most attractive man out here, but I do have a lot to offer. I know you're a single mother and could use some help. I'm a really nice guy and mean no harm. I do thank you for your time and I have enjoyed your company."

He smiled and nodded his head as he stood.

Vivian was speechless. She looked down at the small envelope and then up at the weary look on Leon's face.

Damn, I feel like shit.

"Leon, please sit down?" she asked, reaching for his ringed hand.

Leon didn't take a seat, but he allowed her to hold on to his hand.

"I'm new to all of this. I didn't mean to offend you at all. This is my first date since my divorce. I really didn't know what to expect with all of this. Hell, I didn't expect to meet such a nice guy like you," she explained.

Leon slowly sat back down in his seat with a smug look on his face that confused Vivian.

Is this a game?

For a moment, she felt she was being played.

Vivian picked up the envelope and opened it. It was a spa certificate and two hundred dollar bills. She was appreciative and needed a massage and relaxation. Money was the other thing she needed. Her excitement quickly faded when she pulled out two spa certificates instead of one. She hoped that he didn't plan on going with her.

"You gave me two?"

She waved the two certificates in the air.

"Yes, there is one for you and one for your girlfriend. I thought you might enjoy it more with one of your girlfriends," he said.

"Thank you!" she said, placing the envelope in her handbag and not mentioning the money.

She was relieved that he didn't plan on joining her. Something deep inside her felt that it was wrong to accept his gift so soon. That feeling didn't last long after she thought about how she wouldn't be able to afford a day at the spa on her own.

"Tonight I will be attending a charity auction for breast cancer research and would love for you to join me."

"Tonight isn't good for me. It's short notice and I have children. You would never imagine how hard it is to find a babysitter on such short notice."

Leon smiled, showing his pearly whites. He reached into his back pocket and pulled out his wallet.

"No, Leon."

"This should be enough to convince your babysitter."

He sat a crisp one hundred dollar bill on the table. Vivian looked at the money, and then back at him. She didn't know what to say.

"Yes, but I'm still not sure if I want to go with you tonight. We don't really know each other and I don't want to move to fast."

She tried to let him down easy. She didn't want to go out on a date with him no more than she wanted to be seen with him at the time.

"It's for charity, not for me. My mother is a breast cancer survivor, and I lost an aunt to breast cancer. This event means a lot to my family and me. Most people ignore causes like this until it hits home. Why wait when you can do something about it now?"

He's speech was convincing. If she denied his request, she knew she would feel guilty.

"Okay, I will be there as long as I can get a sitter in time."

"I will pick you up at six o'clock."

"No, I will meet you there. Just send me the address."

"Sure, I will send you the address when I get back to my office. I should be getting back. Now, you get home safely to your children and give me a call later," he said.

They both stood and shook hands awkwardly.

Vivian kicked herself for letting him talk her into going out. It was the talk about his mother and aunt. She couldn't turn down a charity event for breast cancer, especially after his speech.

Vivian allowed Leon to leave first as she felt uncomfortable with the way he spoke about her being a single mother. She didn't want pity from him. She watched him cross the street, get into a black Range Rover, and pull off before she left.

As soon as Vivian got to her car she called Leesa. She kept an eye out for Leon's Range Rover in case he doubled back around.

"How did it go?" Leesa asked.

"Not too great, but the picture was better," Vivian joked.

"Girl, was it that bad?" Leesa asked.

"Yes, but he has a great personality. He actually gave me a gift."

"What did he give you?" Leesa asked.

"He gave me two spa certificates since I'm a single mother."

"Wow! What the hell do you being a single mother have to do with anything? I don't know, he sounds a little weird. What happened to flowers on a first date? Girl, be careful with this one."

"I don't think that it's going to work out. Who still wears S-curls? I did agree to go with him to a charity event for breast cancer tonight."

"You're brave! I have to get going. I'm meeting Doc tonight at my place."

"You didn't tell me that Doc was hitting that!"

"A girl never kiss and tell."

"Since when you didn't kiss and tell?"

"I know right?" Leesa laughed.

"I already know. Have fun for the both of us."

"And you know I will."

Vivian pulled up to the street that led to her home. She checked her rearview mirror several times as her phone buzzed indicating she had an email.

"Hold on, let me check this." Vivian checked her email.

"I think I have another interested party. I just received a message from *DannyBoy804* and he is so handsome. I hope his picture isn't from high school. He either takes care of himself or he is lying about his age."

"Check him out, because this Leon character is not what I had in mind for you. He sounds like he's stuck in the seventies. Gold rings on every finger and a curl out the box. Where they do that at?"

Leesa could hardly get the words out from laughing hard.

Meeting Leon was somewhat discouraging. He wasn't what she had in mind in the looks department, but he was a nice guy. If she was to judge that book by its cover, it would be placed back on the shelf. Now she had another possibility. She was eager to see what *DannyBoy804* was about.

CHAPTER 18

Vivian was dressed for the charity event when the doorbell rang. She wore a black sequenced dress. It was her mother coming over to sit with the children. Her mother was free and the only person available to babysit. She offered her mother money for watching the children, but she wouldn't hear of it.

"Hi, mom," she said.

She kissed her mom on the cheek as the children ran for their hugs from their grandmother.

"You look gorgeous! Who is the lucky guy?"

"It's not a date mom. I don't even like this guy. He invited me to a charity event. I accepted after he made me feel guilty."

"Whatever you say."

Vivian gave her mother the location of the event and all of Leon's information including his license plate that she jotted down.

"Don't let them stay up too late."

"Of course not. You enjoy yourself tonight. Just have fun."

"I will. I love you."

On the way to the *Sheraton Hotel*, Leon called her twice to make sure that she was on her way. He was starting to get on her nerves already. The third time he called, she was parking. She let the call go to voicemail.

Leon was waiting impatiently outside of the hotel. He was pacing back and forth, looking at his watch. Vivian watched him while she crossed the street. It was quarter to seven, in her book that was early.

"What took you so long?" Leon asked.

Vivian stopped dead in her tracks, and then said, "Excuse me?"

"Hello, I'm sorry. It's just that we have to be seated by seven."

"According to my time I'm early. It's not even seven yet."

"I have a little O.C.D. I have to do everything on time. My on time is different from yours."

"A little O.C.D.?"

"Let's get inside. I have our tickets."

He quickly ushered her into the hotel. Vivian was upset with his behavior. She never met anyone with O.C.D. The only thing she really knew was what she saw on television. What she saw made people with O.C.D. look crazy.

She tried to keep a smile on her face as she fumed with anger. They were escorted to their seats. It wasn't until she was finally seated at the table with four others that she was able to take in the scenery.

There were round tables covered in a soft shade of pink. The centerpieces were glass ribbon shaped vases filled with floating pink and white roses. Soft music played in the background as the guest arrived.

Leon seemed more relaxed once they were seated. His shoulders were relaxed and the strain on his face was gone. He introduced Vivian to the other guests at the table. Vivian politely greeted each one of them.

Iced water was placed at each setting. Vivian requested bottle water. She didn't want anything slipped into her drink again. The host of the event was at the podium promptly at seven thirty.

As an introduction, a short film was shown. The film explained breast cancer symptoms, treatments, and the goals of the foundation. The film was narrated by cancer survivors. At the end of the film, they gave a tribute to those who lost their battle with breast cancer. Family members read their names and lit a candle in remembrance of their loved ones.

Everyone was teary-eyed. Vivian even noticed that Leon was fighting back tears. The waiters came by each table and served baked chicken, garlic mash potatoes, and fresh green beans. After the speaker, the auction began.

The auctioneer kept the crowd entertained with his fast talk and humor. Items were donated to raise money for breast cancer research.

"I want to apologize again for earlier," Leon said.

"Thanks for the apology. It was completely uncalled for."

Vivian continued to eat her dinner. This was the first time they had spoken since the program began. She noticed that Leon only ate his green beans.

"Thanks for coming out," he said.

"You're not hungry?"

"I'm a vegetarian."

"O.C.D. and a vegetarian. Leon, you're something else."

The auctioneer began a bid on a sapphire and diamond necklace. It was a beauty. It sparkled from where she was sitting; five tables away.

"That is a beautiful necklace," he whispered in her ear making her feel uncomfortable.

"Yes, it is beautiful."

The bid was at five hundred dollars. There were two people in a bidding war for the necklace, bidding in fifty dollar increments. Leon raised his hand and joined in.

Vivian watched the excitement between the three. The woman dropped out at seven hundred. Leon and a young man went back and forth until Leon outbid him at eight hundred and fifty dollars.

There was an adrenaline rush as she watched the bidders win and lose some. At the end of the night, the bidders claimed their winnings. Vivian waited for Leon as she made small talk with a woman named Mrs. Murphy at her table.

"What's your story?" Mrs. Murphy asked.

"My story? Oh, I don't have one. Are you a breast cancer survivor?" Vivian asked.

"Yes, I am. I had a mastectomy when I was fifty-eight years old. Thank God, my cancer has been in remission for five years."

"Thank God, for that."

"I like to tell young women like yourself to be sure to perform self-breast exams. It's your body and only you can tell when something changes. If you have the slightest lump or change, be sure to let your doctor know."

"I'm so happy that I came here today. I have learned so much about breast cancer."

Vivian couldn't remember the last time she did a self-exam. She counted on her doctor to do them at her doctor visits. That was going to change.

"I'm glad that you came, too."

"I don't have much, but I want to leave a donation."

"Here's an envelope you can leave your donation in. Thank you for your support."

Mrs. Murphy slid an envelope to Vivian.

"Thank you for the inspiration."

She gave a fifty dollar donation thanks to Leon. She felt someone put something over her head and place something cold on her bare chest. She grabbed it and turned around to find Leon. She looked down and saw the beautiful sapphire and diamond necklace.

"No, I can't take this," she said.

"It's yours."

"I can't accept an expensive gift like this from you. We just met. I only came here out of support."

"I came here to support the foundation as well. So I had to bid on something. I don't think it would look as nice on me as it does on you."

Leon had his charming ways. Vivian loved the necklace, but didn't want to give him the wrong idea. She tried to take off the necklace, but he stopped her.

"It's yours and that's the end of it. No strings attached, I promise."

Vivian sighed heavily. Somehow she knew she was going to pay for it. She didn't give him an answer or say thank you. She got up from the table and said goodbye to Mrs. Murphy.

Leon walked Vivian to her car. Vivian speed walked to her car; ready for the night to be over. When she reached her car, she jumped right in. She didn't want him to think she was going to kiss him, because it wasn't a date.

"Thank you. Drive home safely," he said.

"I really enjoyed myself. It felt good to support a great cause."

"Good night."

"Good night," Vivian replied.

Vivian drove away feeling pleased with herself. She put up with Leon for three hours, donated to a cause and came out with a beautiful necklace. She had no intentions on ever seeing Leon again to repay him for his gift.

annyBoy804's message still went unanswered as she tried to wait the three days she set for herself. She didn't want to seem too desperate. The second day, she had to talk to him, especially since her free trial was coming to an end. *DannyBoy804* immediately caught her eye. He was handsome with a beautiful smile. The profile picture was very professional. He was clean cut in a black business suit.

When she finally responded to his message, she didn't have to wait long for a response. He immediately responded. There was an instant connection with him. Vivian found herself extremely attracted to him.

There was the initial greeting and introduction. After greeting one another and having small talk about their day, he asked about her experience on the dating site. He also shared his experiences. The conversation went very well. So well, that it became awkward to address each other with their screen names. He revealed his real name and so did Vivian. His name was Daniel, which wasn't a shock to her. She figured that would be his real name based on his screen name.

Daniel asked to continue their conversation over the phone, she agreed to exchange phone numbers. She found Daniel very interesting. If he turned out to be a psycho, she could easily get her phone number changed.

"Hello?" Daniel answered.

"Hello, Daniel. This is Vivian."

"Hi, Vivian. How are you?" Daniel responded.

"I'm great. How about yourself?"

"I'm blessed. If it's God's will, I will continue to be blessed."

His response surprised her. He sounded like a preacher. She wasn't ready to be a preacher's wife.

"Okay...," she said nervously.

Her excitement was quickly fading.

"I would like to say that I'm not a stalker. I am, who I say I am. Yes, my profile picture is yours truly. It was taken in the past year," he began.

A smile quickly spread across Vivian's face. She relaxed in her chair.

"Well, that's nice to know. I see you have a sense of humor. I'm divorced with three children just like my profile says."

"I'm soon to be divorced, but I don't have any children."

"If you don't mind me asking, why are you getting a divorce? What happened exactly?"

"My wife and I are in two different places. To be honest, we probably should have never married. I worked with her father and he thought that I would be a great son-in-law. My wife is a gorgeous woman, but she is not the woman for me," he explained.

"If you knew that she wasn't the woman for you, then why marry her?" she asked.

She knew that he wasn't completely forthcoming with the reason for his divorce. That was understandable, since they really didn't know each other.

"I loved her, but I knew that we were different. I was young and I thought that she would change. I found out too late that you can't change a person at all. My wife was in love with another man. She only married me to please her father. In the beginning, she tried to make our marriage work. I know that she loved me, but she was in love with someone else. It took five years for us to end it. That's my story."

"That must have been a painful situation for you?"

"Yes, it was for a while. Then it was all business. My father-in-law gave me a piece of the company, and I've worked hard to build a name for myself. I'm now in a place where I can break free and start my own company."

"How does she feel about that?"

"She just wants a clean divorce. We have no ill feelings toward each other. I owe a lot to her father. He understands why we are divorcing, and my reason for moving on with my business. No love lost."

The two of them talked for hours. Vivian told him all about her divorce. Vivian listened; pressing hard against the phone as to get closer to him.

Daniel and Vivian decided to meet for dinner the following weekend. Leesa offered to babysit the children for her. She was excited to finally meet Daniel in person. Leon didn't excite her nearly as much as Daniel. She hoped that this could be something real. There was definitely a connection.

CHAPTER 20

The night was warm with a cool breeze. The skies were bright. Vivian wore her special black dress with a low neck that plunged deep into her lower back. It showed off the cherry blossom tattoo between her shoulder blades.

"You go and have yourself a nice time tonight. Don't worry about us," Leesa said.

"I'll try."

Dominic, Journey, and Demetrius rushed over to their mother. She kissed each one of them and headed for the restaurant.

Vivian arrived at Fleming's twenty minutes earlier than planned. She wanted to get there before her date. She needed her nerves calmed before she decided to change her mind. She sat in the parking lot. *If this is going to be anything like meeting Leon; I'm running for the door.*

She sat in her parked car positioned where she could see people entering the restaurant. She watched men walk into the restaurant alone and wondered if they were

Daniel, but none seemed to favor him. Pulling out her cell phone, she looked at his picture again.

While freshening her makeup in the mirror, she was blinded by bright headlights pulling into the parking space in front of her. She shielded her eyes and frowned. Once she regained her sight, she admired the clean, black shiny Mercedes Benz. She noticed the tinted windows and shiny chrome finish. She received a text from Daniel that read:

I'm at the restaurant. I will meet you inside.

Vivian dropped her lip gloss on her lap when a tall, handsome man exited the car that she was just drooling over. He had on an expensive tailored suit and a diamond watch that blinded her from where she was. It was Daniel. He looked just like his photo, but much better in person.

She watched him straighten his suit and check his phone. He looked her way, but she quickly ducked down in her seat. She waited a few seconds before sitting up. She slowly raised her head. When she sat up, he was gone. She dialed Leesa's number.

"Leesa, I can't do it!" she yelled into the phone.

"You can't do what?" Leesa asked in frustration.

"I can't meet this man. He is out of my league. He is driving a Mercedes Benz and he wears designer suits."

"If you could go on a date with Leon, you could do anything. Have a nice time and don't come back here until your date is over. I mean it!" Leesa said, hanging up on Vivian.

Vivian walked into the restaurant to find a waiting Daniel. He was standing there smiling from ear to ear. Vivian smiled nervously.

"I thought you would never get out the car."

"What?"

She was embarrassed.

"I saw you in the car. I thought you were going to pull off. I don't look that bad, do I?" he asked jokingly.

"Oh, no. I dropped something and bent down to pick it up. You're actually easy on the eyes." she responded.

He took Vivian by the arm as they followed the hostess to their table. Daniel's humbleness and sense of humor relaxed her. Just like a perfect gentleman, he pulled out her chair and placed her napkin on her lap. Daniel took his seat after making sure that she was completely comfortable.

"You have a gorgeous smile."

"So do you. You have yet to stop smiling," she said blushing.

"I'm so glad that you agreed to have dinner with me tonight."

He motioned for the waiter.

"So am I. This is a very nice restaurant. I love it here."

She looked him in the eyes. He was gorgeous.

"Yes, I enjoy it here as well," he agreed.

"Do you bring all of your women here?"

"Do all of your men bring you here?"

They shared a laugh. For the remainder of the night, they talked and shared stories. Vivian was comfortable talking to Daniel. It was as if she'd known him all of her life.

"Well, it seems we are the last ones," he said looking around the restaurant.

"I really didn't notice. I really enjoyed myself tonight. Thank you."

He reached for her hand. They held hands and gazed into each other's eyes for a moment.

"You're more than welcome. I thank you for a beautiful night that I hate to see it end," he replied.

Daniel walked Vivian to her car. She slowly walked back to the car. She didn't want the night to end either. Once they arrived at her car, he opened her car door and waited for her to leave.

He didn't even try to kiss me.

Vivian drove home in bliss. She replayed the night over and over in her mind. Daniel didn't seem like the type that only wanted sex. He seemed interested in getting to know whom she was and the things that made her happy.

Daniel was the type of man she liked. He was handsome, had a career, respectful, and was a good communicator. She enjoyed their conversations and wanted to get to know him better. Things were finally looking up.

CHAPTER 21

Awakened by a ringing cell phone. Vivian rolled over in bed to answer it.

"Hello?" she answered.

"Rise and shine!" Leon said in an overly excited voice.

"What?" Vivian responded.

She sat up in her bed and rubbed her eyes. It was Sunday morning and she had no plans to go out.

"I wanted you to join me at church. It's family and friends day," Leon said.

She hadn't talked to or saw Leon in weeks. She was surprised by his bold tone.

"Leon, I'm not your family or your friend. We don't know each other. You didn't call me to ask about this beforehand. You can't just call the day of and expect me to jump," she said angrily.

"Oh, you will. I have something real special for your time and inconvenience. How did you enjoy the spa? " he asked slyly.

Vivian became very angry when she realized that he thought he could buy her time.

"I'm not for sale, Leon."

"Everybody has a price. I know that you're a single mother. I'm sure that you could use some help. Let's face it, you couldn't afford a day at the spa. You sure couldn't afford a sapphire and diamond necklace."

"I don't need your help, especially if you're going to throw it in my face!"

She was insulted by his blunt words.

"Let's not make this about money. I apologize."

"I don't need your help or anyone else's for that matter. We met once and I haven't spoken to you since. I don't understand how you figure you could impose on me like this."

"Fuck you bitch! I wasted my hard earned money on your ass!" he said angrily.

"You sure did and thanks for the massage and the necklace. Fuck you, too!" she yelled into the phone, hanging up.

Vivian quickly scrolled through her phone to Leon's contact information and blocked his number. She thought about calling Leesa and telling her that she was right about Leon, but decided against it.

Leon's reaction to her rejection opened her eyes to the fact that you really don't know a person when you first meet them. He seemed to be a nice guy. Now that she was starting to see the dark side of internet dating, she decided to be more careful.

CHAPTER 22

I t was Demetrius and Journey's birthday. Timothy called Vivian to ask if he could visit at the house with the children for the weekend. Although, she didn't want him staying at the house, she allowed it for the children. Journey, Demetrius, and Dominic were excited about their father's visit. Vivian was very reluctant, but she knew that the children missed their father and wanted to see him badly. The doorbell rang and the children almost trampled over Vivian. They hadn't seen their father since March.

"Daddy! Daddy!" the children yelled.

Timothy dropped his bags and knelt down to embrace them. Vivian stood nearby with tear filled eyes and joy in her heart. The joy quickly faded when she had a good look at Timothy.

He looked worse than the last time she saw him months ago. She ran into him at their bank unexpectedly. She had no idea he was in town. He had a full beard that was now turning gray. His teeth were stained and the white of his eyes were yellow.

"Children, why don't you let your father get settled in? Go get the cards you made him," she instructed.

Timothy looked up at Vivian in shame. He picked up his duffel bag and suitcase and walked slowly into the house avoiding eye contact.

"Hello, Vivian. How are you?" he asked.

"Hi, Timothy. Have you been drinking? You know that I can't allow you to take the kids out if you have."

She studied him.

"No, I haven't had a drink," he responded.

"Why do your eyes look that way?" Vivian asked.

She walked closer to Timothy. She sniffed the air.

"I said I haven't had a drink! I haven't been doing so well. I lost my job. Samantha and I are over," he said.

"I knew that wouldn't last. Look at how you got the job."

"I don't need you throwing that in my face, okay. I know what I did to you. Trust me, I'm paying for it."

The children returned with their homemade cards and smiles. Timothy's face lit up once again when he saw them.

"Have a good time with your father," Vivian said.

Vivian felt that something wasn't right with Timothy. He looked as if he'd aged ten years. She suspected that more than alcohol was the cause. One bad habit led to another.

After looking out the window to make sure that he and the kids were gone, she began to rummage through his bags. She lifted the suitcase and duffel bag onto the table. Bitterness sat in as she thought back to the day she saw the same duffel bag at her front door.

In the suitcase, his clothes were neatly rolled into small bundles to make more room. She sorted through his pants and shirts. There was nothing other than his toothbrush, deodorant, and shaving kit.

Saving the duffel bag for last, she slowly unzipped it. Sitting on top of wrapped gifts, was a bottle of Hennessy. She grimaced. There were more clothes and toys for the kids. At the bottom of the duffel bag, she found a large plastic bag with two prescriptions. One was his blood pressure medication and the other was Campral.

After researching the prescription online, she found that the medication was prescribed to reduce alcohol cravings, physical distress, and emotional discomfort experienced when a person has quit drinking.

She was glad that he finally sought help for his alcohol addiction. It was evident that he was still struggling with it. She knew all too well about the struggle, watching her mother fight her addiction. She felt sorry for him.

When Timothy and the children returned home, he took the responsibility of getting them ready for bed. Vivian appreciated his help. She made up the sofa for Timothy while he put the children down. She didn't want him to get any ideas about making his way into her bedroom.

While placing an extra blanket on the sofa, she was startled when she heard Timothy behind her.

"I miss this. You and the kids were my world. Now I have nothing," he said.

"You will always have your kids."

He looked at the sofa where Vivian made it clear where he was sleeping.

"Thanks, Vivian."

"What's going on with you? I found Hennessey and alcohol withdrawal medicine in your bag."

"Why are you going through my things? You don't have the right to do that!" he said.

He scanned the living room for his suitcase and duffel

bag. He walked to the front door. When he didn't find them there, he returned to the living room.

"Where are my bags?" he asked.

"They're in the closet."

She walked over to the closet and pulled out both the suitcase and duffel bag.

"I'm worried about you, Timothy. You don't look so good."

"I lost my family, my job, and myself. No matter how many meetings I attend or how many of those pills I take, I still drink," he said.

"You still have your children. Do it for them. They don't need to see their father like this. You have to take care of yourself."

"What about you? Do you still love me?" he asked.

"I will always have love for you, but what we had is gone. I'm not in love with you. Timothy, you have to stop this. Have you looked in a mirror lately?"

"I stopped looking in the mirror a long time ago. After losing you, I couldn't stand it."

"While you're here, please don't drink. If you do, I'm going to have to ask you to leave."

"I understand. Vivian, pray for me," he said.

"I always do."

It hurt to see someone she once loved almost more than herself in so much pain. She gave him a loving hug; assuming that's what he needed. He accepted and expected nothing more.

She truly understood the burden that her father had to carry during the years that her mother almost drank herself into the grave. Never did she see her father get upset and threaten to leave her mother.

Instead, he took on more responsibility around the house and tried to help her stop drinking however he could. He even went as far as searching the house for any hidden bottles of alcohol and poured them down the drain. After a while, that didn't work.

The day her father finally stood up to her mother about her drinking and physically dragged her out of the house was the day that she went to treatment. She was angry at her father for the way he treated her mother that day. At the time, she didn't understand, but later she did.

CHAPTER 23

Vivian met Daniel at *CinéBistro*. She'd worn her red wedges and red and black color blocked sundress. This was her first time at *CinéBistro*. She'd heard about how they served dinner during a movie. She'd seen *CinéBistro* before while shopping at the mall, but never had a chance to check it out.

"Hey, you. Gorgeous as usual," he said.

He hugged and kissed her.

"You're mighty fine yourself."

"You're going to love it here," he said.

He took Vivian by the hand as they walked inside. Their relationship was blossoming. Daniel loved to take her out and spend time with her. She hadn't invited him over to her home yet and she declined offers to go to his place. He was a very considerate person. He always made sure that she was happy and comfortable.

"I heard the *Dark Knight* was a good movie," he said.

"Same here. Who would've thought that both of us were Batman fans," she said with a laugh.

"I've never met another woman that loved Batman as much as I do."

Daniel opened the door to the theater and allowed Vivian to walk in first. They walked over to the bar. The bar was huge. An old, classic black and white movie was projected on the brick wall behind the bar.

"This is cool," she said, as she looked around.

"Would you prefer to sit at one of the tables?" he asked.

Vivian looked around at the tables. There were a few people occupying them.

"No, this is fine. Do we need to get our tickets first?" she asked.

"I already have them. Do you want a drink?" he asked.

"No, thank you."

"Are you going to have something?" she asked.

It was really a test. Daniel told her that he wasn't a drinker. She wanted to see if he would slip up and take a drink.

"No, I don't have a taste for alcohol. I thought I told you that," he said.

"I don't recall that conversation."

Daniel looked at her suspiciously, catching on to what she said.

"Vivian, I really have enjoyed our time together. I've been happier than I've been in a long time," he said.

He took her hand into his and brought it slowly to his lips. He kissed her with warm wet lips. Vivian's eyes closed for a second as she savored the moment. That kiss sent chills up her spine. She hadn't felt that in a very long time. They looked into each other's eyes.

"I feel the same way. I appreciate you taking me out and making me feel special."

"Can I help you?" the bartender asked.

"No, we're fine," Daniel said, and then he looked at his watch.

"Are you ready?"

"For what?"

"It's time for us to be seated for the movie. We can order our food inside."

He held out his arm to help Vivian step down off the barstool just as the call for *Dark Knight* came over the intercom.

"Thank you."

They walked into the theater. Vivian was impressed with the spacious seating. Daniel handed their tickets to a young man that showed them to their seats. They were handed menus.

"This is really nice, Daniel."

"I'm glad you like it," he said.

After briefly looking over the menu, Vivian ordered the crab cake sandwich and Daniel ordered the grilled chicken sandwich. While waiting for the movie or their dinner, whichever came first, they quizzed each other on Batman trivia.

It wasn't long before the lights were dimmed and the previews began. Daniel moved in closer to Vivian. The loveseat styled chairs allowed them the freedom to be as close as they wanted. Vivian nestled into his arms. It felt so good. She felt safe.

The young men and women were still taking orders and bringing them out during the previews. It wasn't long before their order came out. Vivian liked the dinner and movie idea.

After the movie, Daniel walked Vivian to her car. They laughed and talked about the movie on the way. When they got to her car, they stood there in awkward silence.

"I had a great time. The *Dark Knight* was good, but I expected more from Batman," she said sarcastically.

She pretended to show her muscles.

"I did, too," he said, pulling her close to him. "Why don't you come back to my place," he suggested, placing small kisses on her lips.

"No, I don't think so. Not tonight, Daniel."

She was still in his arms as she rejected him. She rubbed his back and moved away from him.

"I have to get back home. I promised Journey I would be there in time to finish reading Charlotte's Web with her," she sighed.

"Well, if you put it that way. I guess it takes the sting off this time," he said jokingly.

She playfully hit him on the arm. She kissed him and drove away with a smile. Daniel was definitely growing on her. It was evident that Daniel wanted to take things to the next level, but she wanted to take things slow. She didn't want to move too fast.

One thing she knew for sure was that the longer she held on to her cookie the better. She really liked him and didn't want him to get the wrong idea about her. If the relationship was meant to be, then he would be patient with her.

CHAPTER 24

Daniel placed the last of his dirty clothes in the hamper. He dragged the hamper across the carpet and quickly tossed it into the laundry room. His condo was on the sixth floor of a newly renovated building. After moving out of his half a million dollar home that he shared with his soon to be ex-wife, he opted for something smaller. There was just enough room for him where he could live comfortably and entertain family and friends if he wanted to.

He was never a neat freak. Since being a bachelor, he'd really neglected to pay attention to his home. He tidied up often, but not often enough according to his part time housekeeper, Carmela.

"Did you want me to set the table or do you want to eat in the living room?" Carmela asked.

She stirred her homemade sauce, scraping the metal spoon against the stainless steel pan.

"What do you think? It's been a really long time since I…" he began.

Carmela stopped stirring and turned to Daniel.

"I will take care of everything. You just get in there and get dressed," she said, pushing Daniel out of the kitchen.

"It smells delicious in here. I can't thank you enough for all of this," he said.

"Uh huh, thank me later with a fat paycheck. I charge extra for cooking." Carmela limped back over to the stove. "When are you going to let me get into that bedroom? You don't have anything I haven't seen before."

"I don't want you doing too much around here. You've done enough."

"I'm not a handicap. I can do anything the rest of you can do and might even be better at it. This limp might slow me down, but it sure don't stop the show."

"I apologize if I made you feel uncomfortable."

"Just don't let it happy again," she said with a wink.

Daniel smiled at Carmela and rushed back into his bedroom to get dressed for his dinner date with Vivian. Things were getting serious between the two of them. He wasn't looking for a serious relationship when he first joined the online dating site. After meeting Vivian, she changed that. She was everything he wanted in a woman. She was beautiful, smart and educated. Although, she was newly divorced it still seemed that she held back her feelings. At times, she seemed to embrace the idea of their relationship going to the next level and other times she seemed more distant and unavailable.

He found himself falling in love with her. She felt right in his arms and in his spirit. He wasn't the pushy type, but he was feeling the need to define their relationship. From his experience, most women would've slept with him ten times over by now. Not Vivian. She was respectable. That made her even more attractive and he desired her.

Carmela set the table for a romantic dinner. She placed a beautiful floral arrangement in the center of the table. Two candles were placed on each end of the table.

The doorbell rang. Daniel opened the door for Vivian. He was speechless. She was absolutely gorgeous. She wore more makeup than usual, but it was nicely done. Her hair was pulled into a sleek bun on the top of her head. She wore a red dress that hugged every curve on her body and sexy high heels.

"Are you going to let me in?" she asked.

"Yes. Come in."

He opened the door wider and stepped back to allow her in. They greeted each other with a passionate and kiss that awakened every nerve in his body.

"You look gorgeous," he said.

"Thank you. You're handsome as always."

"Thanks. Come in. Make yourself comfortable."

Vivian took a seat in the living room. Daniel watched her take in her surroundings.

"You have a lovely place," she said.

"Can I get you some wine or water?" he asked from the kitchen.

"Water is fine, thank you."

There was a sound of clattering pans from the kitchen. Vivian rushed in.

"What was that?" she asked.

When she saw Daniel struggling in the kitchen, she quickly jumped in to help.

"Let me get this," she laughed.

Daniel laughed too.

"I'm supposed to be entertaining you tonight, not the other way around," he said.

"Let me take care of it."

Daniel put his hands in the air and stepped back from the stove.

Vivian jumped in and finished preparing their plates. She placed their meal on the table. Daniel stood by and watched how she moved around his kitchen as if she'd been there before. Although, it was her first time at his home, she seemed to make educated guesses as to where everything was stored. He loved it.

Dinner was quiet and not because there wasn't anything to talk about. It was because Carmela had prepared the best spaghetti and meatballs that either one of them had ever tasted. It was a simple meal that she somehow turned into something more.

"I have really been enjoying spending time with you. Not that I have a lot of it with three children, but the time we spend together is special," Vivian said.

"I agree."

Daniel stopped eating. He looked across the table at Vivian. He reached for her hand. She placed her hand in his.

"I must be honest. I didn't expect for things to get so serious. I can speak myself, that I have feelings for you. I'm not sure how you feel or where you see this going, but I just want to set the record. I want to let you know that I'm feeling you," Daniel said.

Daniel felt Vivian pulling back her hand.

He held her hand tighter and said, "Stop running from me. It's okay to be happy. It's his loss and the next man's gain. You deserve to be loved."

Vivian breathed heavily. It had taken a moment before she could speak.

"As much as those words sound sweet to my ears, it's not that simple. I gave my husband all of me. I was indispensable in my marriage. I loved him and cared for him. In return, he betrayed me. I'm not the same person that I was and I'm just selfish right now," she confessed.

She pulled back her hand and began to eat.

"But how do you feel about me? I know what happened in the past. I want to know how do you feel about us?"

"I like you. I like you a lot. I'm just having a tough time trusting men. To be honest, I'm struggling with some strong feelings. I have so much going on in my life. I'm just not sure if there is room for a serious relationship right now."

Daniel studied her. He knew that was fear talking.

"I understand. I'm a very patient man, and I always get what I want."

"Is that right?" she said seductively.

After dinner, they cuddled together and watched a movie. Just like clockwork, she ended the night before midnight to get home to her children. He asked her to stay the night. As expected, she refused. He really wanted her badly. He could tell that she wanted him too, but fought the urge to let her body lead into a sexual encounter. They both struggled with that. He had feelings for her that grew as they spent more time together. His night ended as usual, with a cold shower.

CHAPTER 25

Vivian and Leesa went to their favorite restaurant, *The Boathouse*. They loved the waterfront view while they enjoyed their food. The water was serene.

They sat on the waterfront deck taking in the scenery. They looked out at the boats. This was their favorite time to come there to see the beautiful sunset. It was priceless.

"I'm glad that you had time come out. You've been really busy lately. But not too busy for Daniel. I knew you were going to find someone on that site. You and Daniel have been spending a lot of time together," Leesa said.

"Since Timothy is here with the children, I figured we could use this time to catch up."

"How is he doing? Is life finally kicking his ass?" Leesa said jokingly.

"I guess he's okay. I didn't really have time to talk to him. The kids were so excited to see him that they left the house as soon as he arrived," she said nonchalantly. There was no way she could tell Leesa that Timothy had lost several pounds. His once smooth caramel skin was now dark and dry. He wore a scruffy beard plagued by grays that covered his mouth.

"Where is this, Daniel? He has us waiting for him and he didn't even call."

"Calm down Leesa. He told me that he would be running late."

She spread her napkin on her lap. She tried to hide her frustration.

"What's the matter with you?" Leesa asked.

"I'm fine. You're starting to make me regret wanting to introduce you to him. I like Daniel a lot. He doesn't try to buy me like Leon. Yet, he still takes me out on dates and buys me the most beautiful flower arrangements every week. He's a perfect gentleman."

"He sounds like a winner. Okay, so what's the problem?" Leesa asked.

"That's the problem! He is the perfect gentleman and someone that I would truly like to be in a relationship with. I'm scared. I didn't expect to find someone like him. I really didn't take it seriously, but I found this man that I can really see myself with," Vivian admitted.

A white speedboat went by. The driver and its passengers waved.

"You aren't ready for a relationship are you? It would be the worst thing that could happen to you," Leesa asked sarcastically.

Vivian tossed a piece of bread at Leesa, missing her shoulder by inches and landing in the water.

"No, I'm not. I don't want to bring any of the baggage from my marriage into a new relationship. I want to trust him and not worry about what he's doing when he's not around me. If I were to consider being in a relationship, I wouldn't mind starting one with him. I'm starting to care for him and it scares me."

"I'm not trying to pressure you into a relationship. If you think that he can be that someone special in your life, then you should pursue it. I'm ready to order." Leesa began looking over the menu.

Just as Vivian looked over her shoulders towards the restaurant, she saw Daniel walking to their table. A smile formed on her worried face.

"What are you smiling for? Sweet baby Jesus, I know that is not Daniel," Leesa said with her mouth wide open and staring.

Vivian turned around to see what Leesa was looking at.

The menu fell to the ground as she straightened in her seat. Daniel stepped out onto the deck behind the waiter. He walked with confidence, but it was not to be mistaken for arrogance.

"Hello, ladies. I apologize for my lateness. My last meeting ran over and I came right away," Daniel said.

He greeted Vivian with a kiss on the cheek. He joined them at the table. Vivian looked over at Leesa, who was staring at Daniel. She gave her a hard kick under the table, jolting her.

"Daniel this is Leesa. Leesa, this is Daniel."

Daniel reached out and shook Leesa's hand.

"I've heard so much about you. I'm glad that we finally have had a chance to meet," Daniel said.

"I'm glad to meet you…" she stumbled over her words.

Looking back and forth at Vivian and Daniel, she gathered herself.

"My apologies again for keeping you ladies waiting," Daniel said.

"No problem," Vivian responded.

Leesa chimed in behind her and said, "No problem at all."

Daniel signaled for the waiter. The waiter came over to take their orders.

"Vivian told me that the two of you have been seeing a lot of each other lately. What are your intentions with my friend?" Leesa asked.

Vivian shot an evil look at Leesa. She was embarrassed by her invasive question. Leesa ignored her.

"Vivian is aware of my situation. I'm looking for a relationship. I prefer spending my time with someone that I can invest in. Vivian and I seem to have the same expectations of each other," he said.

Daniel looked over at Vivian for confirmation. She nodded her head in agreement still glowing.

"How long have you been divorced?" Leesa asked.

Vivian choked on her water. Daniel immediately sprang into action, patting Vivian on her back.

"I'm okay, thanks."

She cleared her throat. Leesa was asking too many questions.

"Leesa, stop asking Daniel all these questions," she said nervously.

"It's okay. I don't mind. I have nothing to hide. My divorce will be final in a couple months, but my marriage was over a long time ago," he explained.

"Oh, so you're still married."

She looked at Vivian suspiciously.

"Leesa is also divorced. She met someone on the dating site. Tell him about Doc," Vivian said, giving Leesa the same look.

"Well, Vivian is not the only lucky one to find someone special online. I believe that I've met my soul mate. He softens my hardness and he breaks down walls that no one has ever managed to do before. He allows me to be me. I'm happy and I'm content."

"Oh, how sweet," Vivian said, pretending to wipe imaginary tears with a napkin.

"That's great," he said.

After their meal, Daniel walked the ladies to their car and ended it with a passionate kiss with Vivian. Vivian was pleased with the way Daniel handled himself. Leesa was just being Leesa. She was her best friend and cared about her.

CHAPTER 26

Dinner ended on a great note, but she dreaded the ride home with Leesa. She was sure Leesa was going to drill her with questions.

Rolling her eyes and climbing into the driver side seat, she said, "Okay, what do you have to say?"

Leesa sat stiffly in her seat. Vivian had driven for ten more minutes before Leesa spoke.

"Daniel is one handsome man. He has his own business and money. I guess you have what you were looking for a *Big Poppa*," she said.

"Yes, he does have money, but it is somehow tied to his father in-law's company. He has the means to provide that's for sure."

"So, he's a married man? I know you're not inflicting the same pain on another woman that was done to you."

"He is technically separated from his wife. His divorce will be final soon. He has his own home and she has her own place," Vivian began to explain.

"You didn't tell me that he was married, Vivian. He is still married until he is divorced, right?" Leesa asked.

"Yes, but that's why we are just friends. In two months, his divorce will be final. He will be free to be with whoever he wants. They have to work out issues with splitting their assets. That's the reason the divorce is taking so long."

"When this divorce is over, is he going to be broke? I'm just asking, because that changes things. I'm just saying."

"I believe they came to an agreement on that. He said that was the only reason why he stayed with her so long."

"Yeah, right. That's what they all say for one reason or the other."

Daniel didn't give Vivian reason not to believe the things he told her about his marriage. She still couldn't be sure that it was exactly the way he said things were.

"We are just friends. Once he gets his divorce, maybe we can work on building something. I just don't know right now. I have too many problems. I have the hardest time finding a job in this dead economy and paying my bills."

Vivian pulled into Leesa's driveway and kept the car running.

"I think he knows that you've been through a lot. He has to understand that it is going to take time for you to want a serious relationship. You definitely need some help in the sex and financial areas of your life."

"Yes, I need my mortgage paid and some more," Vivian joked. "Seriously, I thought about propositioning him. He can get what he wants, and I could get what I need. Does that make me sound like a prostitute?" Vivian asked.

"Yes it does, but you would be one expensive lay," Leesa said jokingly. "On a more serious note, if I had it I would give it to you."

"You've done more than enough for me and my family. You've helped with the children and loaned me money on several occasions. I really appreciate everything you've done for me," Vivian told her.

They shared a hug. Leesa exited the car. Vivian rolled down the passenger's side window when she saw Leesa heading back to the car.

"What girl?" Vivian asked.

"If you don't want him, you can pass him on to me."

"What would the good doctor think about that?" Vivian asked.

"What the good doctor doesn't know won't hurt him."

"Leesa, you're so crazy! Go in the house."

"Really, Vivian? I think that you should give him a chance. Make him your man and you can get it all."

"Yeah, I just might."

On her way home, she contemplated the rest of her weekend with Timothy visiting. As the father of her children, she was worried about him. She planned to help him put in applications online and support him during his sobriety.

CHAPTER 27

Vivian was up all night faxing and emailing her resume to companies that were hiring. After searching for jobs in the newspaper and online, finding full time work was wearing her down. She was starting to think that she wasn't going to find a job. The kids were heading back to school and she needed to find something fast.

"Mom, the mailman is at the door!" Journey yelled.

"I'm coming!" Vivian yelled from her bedroom.

She grabbed her robe and rushed to the door.

"Good morning. Sign here," the mailman said, handing her an envelope.

"Thank you."

The mailman nodded and continued on his route. Vivian read the envelope. It was from her mortgage company. It was a letter demanding that she make her three missed mortgage payments before foreclosure proceedings began. She read the letter in its entirety before balling it up in frustration.

"How am I supposed to come up with all of this money in the next thirty days!" she yelled.

She thought about calling her parents for the money, but she couldn't ask them again. The only person that could possibly give her the money was Daniel. Lately, Daniel's sexual advances had become more frequent. The fear of having her heart broken made her suppress her true feelings for him. Daniel was what she wanted in a man, but her immediate needs outweighed her wants.

Vivian came up with a plan to give Daniel what he wanted and to get what she needed. At that moment, she decided that she was going to put her plan in motion.

CHAPTER 28

Vivian invited Daniel over for dinner. The children were over Leesa's house for the night. She prepared Daniel's favorite meal consisting of steak, vegetable medley, and baked potato.

The plan was to have dinner and during their conversation, she would insinuate that she was willing to trade sex for money. Based off his response, she would say either she was joking or she would go for it. The plan could blow up in her face sending Daniel out the door or it could save her home.

Daniel arrived casually early as usual. Vivian knew this and was ready for his arrival.

"You have a beautiful home. It smells great in here. You must have one special evening planned," Daniel said.

This was his first time inside of the house. He took in his surroundings.

"Thanks, it's hard keeping it that way with children running around here. Dinner is ready. The bathroom is down the hall on the left," she announced from the dining room.

When Daniel returned, she poured herself a glass of wine.

"Everything looks great," he said.

"Thank you. Have a seat so we can eat," she said in a sexy voice.

"Wow, this is a side of you I've never seen before. I love a woman that can cook," he said.

He walked over to the dining room table and took a seat.

"This is my favorite, but I think I have a new favorite; you," he said.

He reached for her, but she pulled away.

"No sweets before dinner."

"I will be sure to save room for dessert then," he said with a sly grin.

Vivian hoped that her plan would work. She wasn't sure how Daniel would take her offer. All she knew was that if she didn't come up with the money needed to save her house, her and her children would be on the streets.

After dinner, Vivian cleared the table. Daniel finished his sweet tea in the living room as soft jazz played in the background.

CHAPTER 29

Vivian rinsed the dishes and put the remainder of the food away. She took her time doing so as she talked herself into going through with her plan. When she was done, she joined Daniel in the living room with a glass of wine.

"Everything was delicious. I could definitely get used to this," he said.

She was beginning to get nervous and contemplated backing out of her plan. She began to get butterflies in her stomach as the night was ending.

"I have a proposition for you," she began.

She could feel her hand begin to shake as she reached for Daniel's hand.

"I'm listening," he said, licking his lips.

He moved closer to her.

"I'm in a financial bind. I may lose my house if I don't catch up on my mortgage payments. There is no way that I'm going to end up on the streets with my children. I'm willing to do anything to keep a roof over their heads."

The nerves she had minutes ago quickly abandoned her. She began to regret her words. She tried to pull away from him, but he held her hand tightly.

"Why didn't you tell me you were going through this?"

"It's not your problem. I'm sorry that I even invited you over here for this."

She yanked her hand from him and leaped off the sofa.

"Now hold on. I didn't say you did anything wrong. I just wished you had told me that you were having financial problems. It seems that you did all of this to get me here and then lay this on me."

"I'm willing to sell myself to you for money. I would say that something is wrong with that. I don't know what I was thinking doing this."

She tried to leave the living room, but he blocked her path. They stood there looking into each other's eyes.

"Vivian, I'm not sure what's happening here. I didn't know that you were going through all of this. Why didn't you tell me?" he asked again.

"I didn't know how."

"What if I said that I will take you up on your offer? I will make love to you, and you wouldn't have to worry about losing your home."

Vivian stepped back in disgust now that he propositioned her. Suddenly, he didn't seem like the kind gentleman she came to know.

"This is not what I expected. I went about this all wrong."

"I'm going to give you an answer to your proposition. I will give you what you need for your house as a friend. I want to be with you, Vivian. It's not just about sex for me. You should know that by now," he said.

Vivian had the answer she was looking for. She would

give Daniel what he wanted and she would get what she needed.

She was hesitant at first, struggling with her emotions. He took her into his arms and wiped the tears that fell to her cheeks. He kissed her softly. She took him by the hand and led him to her bedroom.

Vivian began breathing heavily as he licked her lips a few times, teasing her with his tongue. They kissed deeply. He laid her on the bed. His kisses moved from her mouth to her neck in circular motions. She moaned and ran her fingers across his back and lifted his shirt over his head. He removed his pants.

Slowly, he removed her clothing, piece by piece. Grinding his pelvis into hers, sliding his manhood back and forth and stimulating her. She pushed back craving him inside of her. Her moans grew louder.

Vivian shook nervously as she anticipated his next move. She let him lead. He sucked on her nipples and took in as much of her C-cups into his mouth as he could. He sucked hard sending both pain and pleasure as he slid his tongue from side to side moving between her breast and down to her stomach.

She reached for his head, running her fingers through his hair. He licked and kissed the insides of her thighs finding his way to her center. Vivian erupted into moans of pleasure as the wet sounds reverberated with the powerful sensations that ran all over her body.

"I want you inside me!"

At her request, Daniel worked his way back up to her breast. He first rubbed himself against her, and then slid slowly inside. They moaned in unison as tides of pleasure overwhelmed them both. He buried his head into her neck. She cried out. She quickly placed her hand over her mouth to muffle her moans. She'd never felt such pleasure before. He moved her hand from her mouth and kissed her. He slid in and out of her until they both exploded in ecstasy.

The next morning, she was awakened by Daniel to breakfast in bed. He fixed cheese grits, sausage, and toast. He handed her a plate of food.

"Thanks, Daniel." She avoided eye contact with him.

She sat up in bed. She took a bite of her toast. She didn't have much of an appetite. She still couldn't believe what happened. Her head was still spinning from the night before. Sex with Daniel was amazing. It was the best sex she'd ever had. She thought that sex with Timothy was mind blowing at times, but Daniel proved her wrong. She was satisfied sexually, but felt ashamed of her actions. She regretted the proposition.

"I wanted to do something special for you," Daniel said, placing a kiss on her cheek.

She gave him a small smile.

"My kids will be home soon."

"Oh, okay. I guess I better get out of here then."

She could tell that he wasn't ready to leave, but she didn't care.

"Yes, I guess you better."

Daniel picked up his neatly folded pants and shirt he placed on the armchair in the bedroom. He went into the bathroom to get dressed.

Once she heard the bathroom door close, she pulled the covers over her head and screamed into the pillow. When Daniel came out, she sat up and put on a smile. He walked over to the bed, sat beside her, and kissed her.

"I had a great time," he said.

"Me, too. Let me see you to the door."

Vivian walked Daniel to the door and opened it.

"I see you're in a hurry. I'll give you a call later."

"Sure."

She pushed the door to close it. Daniel stuck his arm inside of the door.

"I wanted to tell you that I called your mortgage company. I kind of went through your mail. You shouldn't have to worry about a payment until next month."

"You did? Thank you, but you really didn't have to," she said hesitantly.

She was not proud of how she was able to have those payments made.

"But I did. Next time you need something, don't be afraid to ask. I wouldn't want to see you or the kids…" he began.

"Look, Daniel. I'm sorry. I shouldn't have brought my problems to you the way that I did." She closed the door.

Vivian walked back to her bedroom and fell flat on her bed.

What the hell did I do?

Her financial issues were temporarily fixed, but she may have just ruined a potential relationship for it.

CHAPTER 30

hree weeks passed since she last saw or spoken to
Daniel. Daniel's feelings didn't seem to change from
their sexual encounter. He called her frequently and
sent flowers weekly to her home, just as he did
before they had sex. Vivian avoided all of his calls and
refused his weekly flowers. She was too ashamed of her
actions to face him. Eventually, the flowers stopped, and
then his calls became less frequent. Vivian kicked herself
every time she thought about Daniel and the foolish
move she made. She missed him a lot, but felt that there
was no coming back from what she did.

Vivian received a call back for a second interview
from a company offering her a salary that would be more
than enough to take care of her needs. The first interview
went well enough for her to be called back for a second
interview. She had high hopes for this one. It was in her
field with room to grow.

There were three other people there for the interview.
No one said anything to each other. Each person was

called for their interview individually. Vivian was the last to be called.

The receptionist led Vivian to a nearby conference room. There were four people sitting on the opposite side of the large table. They were all in conversation when the receptionist announced Vivian.

All four of the interviewers acknowledged Vivian's presence.

"Good afternoon." She stopped in mid-sentence.

The interviewer at the end of the table was Daniel. Vivian's words were stuck in her throat. She couldn't move. Daniel was the last person she expected to see.

"Is everything all right?" the female interviewer asked.

"Yes," she managed to say in a shaky voice. "I left something in my car."

She quickly turned on her heels and rushed out of the conference room. When she reached the elevator doors, she could hardly breathe.

"Vivian, where are you going?" Daniel called behind her.

Vivian desperately pressed the elevator button. She didn't respond, keeping her back turned to him.

Daniel was almost to her when the elevator doors opened. Vivian stepped into the elevator and saw Daniel running to her. She pressed the button for the lobby as the doors began to close on Daniel.

When she made it to the lobby she dashed out of the elevator. She was in tears as she realized that she was not going to get her dream job.

She ran out of the building. Almost to her car, she heard Daniel calling out to her. She ignored him and continued through the parking lot.

"Vivian, stop! Let me talk to you!"

When Daniel finally caught up to her, he was out of

breath and holding his side from apparently running down the four flights of stairs. He grabbed her arm.

"Please let me go. I didn't know that you worked here."

She nervously tried to open her car door, but couldn't due to her hands shaking violently. The cool winds whipped hard against their bodies. Daniel pulled his suit jacket tight against his body. Vivian wrapped her scarf tightly burying herself deeper into her coat. The sharp, brisk wind stung her face causing her to turn from the direct hit of the wind. He stood between her and her escape. He leaned against the driver side door preventing her from getting inside. With every breath, steamed clouds filled the air.

"Please come back and finish the interview. Don't let me stop you."

"No, I don't think so. I can find something somewhere else. I have to go."

Daniel stood in between Vivian and her car. He fought desperately to catch his breath.

"Are you all right?" she asked.

"This is one of the companies that I have. We are merging. I'm still on the panel to help fill new positions. After all the positions are filled, I will no longer reside on the board. So don't let me stop you from getting this job."

"I can't go back in there. I was so embarrassed when I saw you. I just didn't know what to do."

"Vivian, trust me. The job is yours. The other candidates have been ruled out. If you want, I will remove myself from the panel. Just go back and finish the interview."

"No!" she yelled, as she pushed him away.

"Think about your children, Vivian."

Vivian took a deep breath and considered what she

would be up against if she was to leave. She needed the job badly. If she walked away, she could be making a big mistake. She didn't want to live with any more regrets.

"Okay, I'm going. I have to do this for my children."

"Thank you," he said, breathing heavily.

"Are you all right?"

"Yeah, I'm just out of shape."

"Do you think they will see me after running out of there?"

"You told them that you left something in your car, right? Forget about what happened between us, and think about your children. You need this job."

"Yes, I guess I better get back in there," she said hesitantly.

Her children were her strength, and he reminded her of that.

"Knock'em dead," he said.

"I will."

Vivian quickly turned on her heels and rushed back towards the building. When she got to the front doors, she turned and said, "Thanks, Daniel, for everything."

He waved her off with a smile. He leaned on the vehicle still huffing and puffing from his four flight run.

When Vivian arrived on the fourth floor, she was surprised to find the receptionist waiting for her.

"The panel is taking a break. They will be ready for you in fifteen minutes."

"Thank you."

Vivian took a seat in the waiting area. She took the time to gather herself and focus on the task at hand. She said a prayer, put a smile on her face, and gained her confidence back.

Vivian was called into the conference room. She took a seat at the conference table. After being informed that one of the panel members was not going to be able to attend the interview, the panel decided to move forward.

Vivian was offered the position on the spot. The offer was one she couldn't refuse. She thanked each one of the interviewers. She tried to keep her excitement contained until she left the conference room. She almost hugged the receptionist. This was just what she needed for her family, a new start. She called Leesa.

"Leesa, I have the job! They offered me more than I expected! Thank you, Jesus!" Vivian yelled into her cell phone.

"Congratulations! I told you this one was yours. I'm so happy for you, Viv."

"You're not going to believe who was on the interview panel. Daniel!"

"Daniel? Is that one of his companies?"

Vivian filled Leesa in on the day's events, sparing no details. Vivian headed out of the building, and then to her car. From a distance, she could see that someone left something on her car. As she came closer, she saw that it was a bouquet of flowers and a card. Cautiously, she approached her car.

"Let me call you back. Someone left flowers on my car."

"It's probably Daniel. You're one blessed woman."

She hung up her cell phone and picked up the flowers and card, a voice startled her.

"I love you, Vivian," Daniel said.

"Daniel! What is all of this?" she asked nervously.

"Let's start over. What happened in the past is in the past. We have something special. I miss you."

"Daniel, I don't think…" she began.

"Just because your marriage didn't work, doesn't mean that you can't find happiness. You're a good woman. You deserve a man that will appreciate, love, and respect you."

"So, you don't think I'm a gold digger?" she asked.

She looked into his eyes in search of the truth.

"I know that you're a woman who loves her family. You did what it took to provide for your family. There was a downturn, and you were determined to find your way up, and out of that situation. I respect that," he said.

Vivian felt better after hearing what Daniel had to say. Daniel pulled her close to him. She looked down at the ground. He lifted her chin.

"I'm sorry for treating you that way," she said tearfully.

"I love you, Vivian!"

"I love you, too, Daniel."

Vivian and Daniel embraced each other as she shed tears. She let go of the pain that Timothy caused her, financial hardship, and self-pity. She finally would have a career she could be proud of and a man who professed his love for her.

EPILOGUE

Vivian was at her happiest in many years. Daniel proposed and she accepted. They eloped to Las Vegas and celebrated with a grand reception with family and friends upon their return. He was great with Dominic, Demetrius, and Journey. The children liked him and she loved him. She made it clear how important her career was, and that she was not going to quit her job under any circumstances. This time, she was going to do things her way, and not have a man dictate her life. Daniel had no problem with Vivian wanting to work outside of the home. He respected her for making that decision.

She'd achieved her career goal as a human resource manager. Along with her earlier years of experience, master's degree, and excellent job performance, she received an early promotion. After only seven months on the job, she was promoted to director.

Timothy moved back to Richmond to partner with a former colleague in a software development venture. He had been sober for five months. Drinking was no longer at the forefront of his mind. Thinking with a sober mind, he focused on his career and building a relationship with his children. He and Vivian were able to come to mutual grounds for the sake of the children. As parents, they would set aside their feelings about each other and put the children first.

Samantha was in a horrible car accident on her way to work one morning; leaving her paralyzed from the neck down. She had elderly parents and a sister that didn't want the responsibility of caring for her. She was sent to a special care facility where she would spend the remainder of her days.

James was living in Atlanta where he established a successful practice. However, he was found dead. He hung himself after facing charges for the rape and sexual assault of two of his employees.

Vivian and Leesa maintained their close relationship. Although, both their lives were evolving, they remained close. Great things were happening for the both of them. Leesa was expecting her first child, something she'd wanted for a very long time. They often laughed at the fact that they both found love on the internet, in the most unlikely way.

www.ingramcontent.com/pod-product-compliance
Lightning Source LLC
Chambersburg PA
CBHW050448110726
47899CB00003B/861